THE

Bad Date

DIARIES

JILLY DU PLESSIS

This book is dedicated to my cousin, Tamaryn, whose hilarious foray into the world of online dating inspired much of this book.

ACKNOWLEDGEMENTS

This book wouldn't exist without the support of my husband, who believes I can do anything and makes me believe too. And my two precious girls, who are infinitely patient when mommy is in her writing cave.

CHAPTER ONE

MY OVARIES are about to shrivel up and die. At least, according to my mum they are. Apparently, that's what happens when you turn thirty.

I love her dearly but the woman is a bit of a drama queen. I've just endured a thirty-minute telephone call from her asking if I'm still single and listing all the reasons why I need to settle down and start a family, not least of which is the state of my ovaries.

I think her exact words were, "Catherine, you know it's all downhill once you turn thirty? Declining fertility. I read all about it. Your ovaries are going to shrivel up like prunes. There's no time for faffing about, darling. We need to find you a husband."

Wouldn't she be surprised to know that I'm currently rushing around like a madman because her phone call has made me late for a blind date?

Surprised is not the right word. Horrified is a more accurate term.

I was a bit appalled myself when my cousin Clementine suggested online dating.

"Where is it?" I mutter to myself, as I fly around the room trying to find the black dress that I had in my hands a few minutes ago. I rifle through the piles of discarded dresses that are sprawled all over the bed.

"Yes!" I give myself a mental fist pump as I locate the dress and scramble to get it on. I hate being late. I also hate the mess, but there's no time to tend to both, and being punctual matters far more right now.

The problem with being an only child is that there is all this pressure on you to settle down and procreate. Especially when you're from a well-to-do family where words like "legacy" and "heritage" are frequently thrown around.

During the call, my mother also informed me that her death is imminent because she is so very old (she's not) and if I really loved her, I'd give her a grandchild who is sure to keep her mind young and healthy.

She also read an article saying that grandparents who babysit their grandchildren regularly are less likely to develop Alzheimer's.

I'm not sure how that will work exactly when she lives in England and I've just moved to America, but in true Felicity Callahan style, she wasn't about to be bogged down with the details while delivering her speech.

While my dramatic mum might induce some eye-rolling, the truth is that since I turned twenty-nine last week, I really have been feeling a bit like an old maid.

Thirty is fast approaching and I'm nowhere near settling down. I thought at the very least I'd be married by thirty. Instead, I've spent the last ten years building a career I'm proud of. I've had some short-term, casual relationships here and there, and one more serious relationship that ended in disaster.

When friends ask if I'm single I always joke, "I prefer independently owned and operated". I haven't really felt that I needed a man. Until recently, that is.

After things ended with Johnny, I was content single. But these days I look at Clem and her husband, Dan, and their twins, and I feel pangs of benign jealousy because I also want that. I want a man who will look at me the way Dan looks at Clem. I want a family.

I'm too young for a mid-life crisis. Is there such a thing as a quarter-life crisis? I think I'm having one. It must be because, in spite of feeling the pressing need to settle down, it's the only reason I'd agree to something as crazy as online dating. I like order and control, and doing something like online dating is way, way out of my comfort zone.

I'd told Clementine it was a bad idea, but she reassured me that it's dating in the 21st century and it would help me to loosen up a bit. Where else was I going to meet a man?

As Clem had gently pointed out, I spend most of my time working and there are no eligible bachelors at work.

This is true. Aside from one fresh-faced co-worker named Todd, who's way too young for me, the only men at work are either old, married, or gay. Or all of the above, and considering I've only been living in America for five weeks, these are really the only men I've spent any time with.

"Was that Lady Floss on the phone?" Clem asks as she appears at the door of her guest bedroom, which is where I'm currently staying until I find my own place.

My mum doesn't really have the title of Lady, but she comes from a long line of British aristocrats and certainly behaves as if she is part of the Peerage. Her snooty ancestors are probably rolling in their graves at the knowledge that she married an Irishman! That thought always gives me a little chuckle.

Thankfully, she also has a great sense of humor so when shameless Clem calls her "Lady Floss" to her face, Mum just clucks and shakes her head. I think she secretly quite likes it.

"Yes. She was reminding me that I'll be too old to give her grandchildren if I don't settle down soon. My fertility is apparently on the decline and she needs a grandchild to prevent her from getting Alzheimer's…or something like that. Zip me up, please?" I reply as I stand in front of the mirror and start on my hair and make-up.

I glance at Clem through the mirror.

"Remind me why I'm doing this again?"

"Uh, because you don't want your mum to try and arrange a marriage for you?" Clem laughs at the thought because she knows it is entirely plausible. Just before I started dating Johnny, Mum tried to set me up with the son of one of her bridge club friends. Clementine is spot on. I'd rather not have a repeat of that disaster.

"Where do normal people meet men, Clem? A bar?"

"Kate, the only men you're likely to meet at a bar are ones just looking for a good time." She huffs as she finishes zipping me up.

"True, but there are plenty of those on dating apps too— probably more so. And married ones at that," I argue. She clearly hasn't thought that argument through properly. I suck in a breath as a terrible thought crosses my mind. "Or worse…serial killers."

My mascara wand is suspended above my eyelashes as I try to process what a monumentally bad idea this really is.

"I don't want to end up cut into little pieces in somebody's basement Clem!"

"You know sometimes you're as dramatic as your mother? That's why you only meet in public places, Kate."

She rolls her eyes and folds her arms over her ample chest. She's a knock-out. No wonder Dan was smitten the moment he met her. He'd come to the UK on a business trip and fell hard for her. It was quite amusing watching Dan "the man" relentlessly pursue Clem when she wasn't all that impressed by him. Of course, he got the girl in the end and they are sickeningly sweet together.

Clementine calling me dramatic is a little bit rich. I may be a little high strung, but Clementine likes a bit of drama and gossip as much as my mother does. Our mothers are sisters. I think it's in the genes.

I twist to look at myself from all angles.

"Do you think I look okay?"

"You look gorgeous. You always do you silly goose."

"Not too low-key?" I ask. "I mean it's a little black number but it's not exactly a cocktail dress."

I glance down at the loose-fitting dress that ends mid-thigh. Eighteen years of dancing means I have a ballerina's legs—long and strong, but are you supposed to wear something so short at this age?

"Do you think I'm too old to wear this type of thing?"

Clementine fixes narrowed eyes on my head and reaches toward me.

"Oooh, is that a gray hair I see?"

I bat her hand away and glare at her now-grinning face.

"You really will start giving yourself gray hairs if you don't stop stressing, Kate. I told you, The Old Copper Pig is perfect for a first date and you look just fine. It's a pub-style restaurant, not a cocktail dress sort of place anyway."

"The name is a bit odd."

"It's charming. I promise, you're going to love it. The food is great and you'll love the décor. It's also fairly busy, which is why it's perfect for a first date. Lots of witnesses."

"Clem!"

The implication of a crime occurring on my date is not doing my nerves any favors. I feel like Mrs. Bennet, and am tempted to shout, "Nobody feels for my poor nerves"—although if I'm being honest, my mother is probably closer to Mrs. Bennet than I am, as the current purpose of her life definitely is to get her daughter married.

I style my wayward brown curls as best I can, grab my heels, and make my way downstairs with Clem on my tail.

"Wish me luck," I say as I turn and give Clem a kiss on the cheek before heading down her front steps. "If I'm not home within a few hours I'm probably being turned into a skin suit."

"Melodramatic." I can hear Clementine laugh as she closes the front door.

CHAPTER TWO

I TAKE a deep breath to try calm my roiling stomach as I step through the doors of The Old Copper Pig. The blast of warm air is a welcome relief from the chilly breeze outside.

As my eyes scan the surroundings, I'm struck by how light and welcoming the place is. With a name like The Old Copper Pig and the Irish-style pub exterior, I was expecting a dark and dingy place, not this.

To my right, a long bar runs the length of the room, with mason jar pendant lights overhead. Behind the bar, bottles of liquor stand proudly against the exposed red brick wall, and the high ceiling is composed of exposed steel beams.

There are natural wood tables spread out around the room, adorned with small succulent centerpieces, and surrounded by distressed creamy yellow leather chairs that look incredibly comfy. I notice that at the top of each skewer that indicates the table number is a little copper pig. The whole place is a trendy mix of rustic and industrial. The wannabe-designer in me is delighted. Clem was right, it's gorgeous.

Just like the bartender wiping down glasses.

Well, hello handsome!

My eyeballs can't help but do a happy little dance down the length of his body. At least, what I can currently see of it. It's like I have no control over them. I also seem to have no control over the contented sigh that slips out.

He is gorgeous. I know I shouldn't be objectifying him like this, and restraint is usually my middle name, but I just can't help it.

Like the second bartender serving drinks at the far end of the bar, he's wearing a white dress shirt, only hot guy's sleeves are rolled up to his elbows. I can see his impressive biceps flexing under the white cotton as he works. I mentally slap myself.

Focus Kate. You're here for a blind date, not to ogle the bartender.

"Welcome to The Old Copper Pig. Do you have a reservation?"

I'm so busy drinking in the bartender that I give a startled little yelp at the waiter who seems to have appeared out of nowhere. He should have a bell attached to him. My cheeks must be a lovely shade of crimson right now.

"Hi. Sorry. Yes, I do. Kate Callahan." I wonder if he noticed me eyeing the bartender. I decide to play it cool by scanning the room again. "I'm just waiting for somebody. He should be here soon."

Thanks to the efficient T, I surprisingly managed to get here right on time. Yay for public transit systems that actually run on time!

The waiter does a quick scan of a book at the entrance.

"Ah, yes. We've got a table for you when you're ready. Would you like to get a drink at the bar while you wait?"

And get a closer inspection of the hot bartender? Can't say I'm opposed to enjoying some eye-candy while I wait.

"That would be lovely, thank you," I say as I make my way over to the bar.

The bartender seems to be looking at me approach, but it's a faraway look. Like perhaps he's not really registering what he's looking at. As I take a seat on the high-back bar stools the bartender seems to snap out of his trance as he straightens his back and looks me directly in the eyes.

His dark hair is sticking up in a few different directions, as if he's yanked on it. There's something about that bed-head look that's quite endearing.

He clears his throat. "Hi. What can I get for you?"

This close, I can see he has the most beautiful blue-green eyes, like the sea after a storm. So expressive. And his voice—deep and smooth, without the traditional Boston twang that I've grown accustomed to in the past few weeks.

I'm so busy fawning over him that it takes me a few seconds to register that he had asked me a question, so I blurt out the first thing that comes to mind.

"Uh… wine?"

Kate you fool! You don't even like wine!

I don't drink very much alcohol, except those fruity cocktails, and I definitely don't drink wine. It was just the first thing that popped into my head.

Clearly, my brain is not firing on all cylinders when in close proximity to such hotness. And now it's too late to correct my little blunder. It reminds me of panicking in the queue at a sandwich shop and ending up with a distressing combination of fillings. I really should take more time to think things through. I'm usually more confident, but every now and then I'm so socially awkward it's painful.

"Do you want to try Three Brothers? It's a Moscato."

I'm ashamed to say that this well-bred English girl has no clue what a Moscato even is, but I can't exactly tell him that I don't really like wine, now can I? After I literally just asked for wine, he'll think I'm a nutjob. Besides, I'm not about to turn down anything this gorgeous specimen is offering.

"That sounds fine, thank you."

"I'm Ben by the way." Bartender Ben. It suits him.

"Hello, Ben. I'm Catherine, but my friends call me Kate," I reply.

I want to say more but my confidence has deserted me and my mouth is ignoring my brain's instructions to say *something. Anything.*

"You have a British accent, Kate. Are you here on vacation?" Ben's question saves me from an awkward silence as he pours the wine before getting back to cleaning the wine glasses that he was busy with when I sat down.

Ben is not only handsome, he's also observant.

"No. I actually just moved here from London for work five weeks ago."

Not wanting to look like an idiot, I take a tiny sip of my drink. I never thought I'd say this about wine, but it really isn't bad—it's fruity and much sweeter than any wine I've tasted.

"That must be a bit of a culture shock. I spent a summer backpacking through Europe with my brothers after college. I loved it. The history, the culture…everything. As much as I love Boston's rich history, the American people and culture couldn't be more different than over there. I imagine that's taken some getting used to."

I chuckle, although inwardly I'm delighted that the notion of acclimating to a new culture has even crossed his mind. Typically, when people learn I'm from England, their initial comments don't revolve around how well I'm adapting to cultural differences. He's thoughtful.

"Well, it *is* very different, but everybody has been very welcoming. It was a transfer with a global PR company, Pied Piper PR, so I already knew a few faces from the Boston office, which helps."

"Bostonians are great." He winks which makes me giggle like a schoolgirl.

Get a grip Kate.

"They are, but I notice you don't have the accent. Did you grow up around here?"

"Not exactly. Have you heard of Martha's Vineyard?" At my nod, he continues. "I grew up in a little place called Edgartown. It was always peaceful in the off-season, and in the summer, we'd spend our days on South Beach or biking around the island." He sighs and there's a wistful look in his eyes. "The Vineyard is great. Crazy busy in the summer, but great. You should visit it sometime."

"You sound like you miss living there."

"Yes and no. It was an idyllic childhood, but I love the hustle and bustle of Boston too. Plus, I do visit the Vineyard fairly often. My parents still live in the house I grew up in. I've got the best of both worlds, so I can't complain. How about you? You've been here five weeks, huh? Are you missing your family yet?" he asks.

"No! Definitely not."

I temper the emphatic statement with a grin so he doesn't think I'm a terrible person who hates her family.

"I adore my mum and dad, but my mum can be rather…overbearing. Sometimes a little bit of distance is good. Even more so now that she's on my case to settle down and start a family."

I mentally kick myself for getting personal so quickly. Nobody would guess that a publicist who spends all day speaking to people is so socially awkward.

I'm a chronic overthinker in these situations, replaying conversations in my head, which begins a nasty cycle of post-event ruminations. *What clever response should I have given instead? Why didn't I say this or that? What did they think when I said that?*

I really need to pull myself together. I feel a bit better with my over-share when Ben replies.

"I feel your pain. My mother's been on my case to settle down for at least three years."

"Ah, so you're an expert. Any advice on how to deal with that?"

I had noticed he doesn't wear a wedding ring and I'm dying to know if he has a girlfriend, but it would be rude to outright ask.

He gives me a knowing smirk as if he can read my thoughts and simply says, "There's nobody special in my life at the moment so it's a moot point."

"But is it something you want? I mean, is that on the cards for you?"

Before I can stop myself the words tumble out of my mouth. I give myself another mental kick. He probably thinks I'm an absolute nutter. I only just met the guy and I'm asking if he wants to get married. *Ground, swallow me now!*

"It's a serious commitment. I'm definitely not in any hurry to settle down."

This thrill I felt at hearing he didn't have a girlfriend is quickly replaced by disappointment. The news settles in my stomach like a stone. I don't know why. It's not like Ben is my blind date after all. I need somebody who is looking for something serious. I don't plan to go racing down the aisle or anything, but it should at least be on the horizon.

I really like Ben. He's easy to talk to, plus it doesn't hurt that he's so easy on the eyes. He looks about my age, perhaps a few years older, and usually when a guy so hot it should be illegal is still single, it's not for a lack of options. That ushers in an unwelcome thought— maybe he's a bit of a player. Not that it matters.

Sadly, he doesn't fit *the list*. Even without my mum's promptings, I decided a few weeks ago that with thirty on the horizon I don't have time to dilly dally, so I made a checklist. I need somebody with a good, stable job who can support a family.

The ex, Johnny, was an absolute mooch who tried to wring me dry. He had a part-time job that barely covered his rent and spent most of the week on his PlayStation.

Like the sucker that I am, I was sweet-talked into paying for all our meals out, activities, trips. His friends used to call him Johnny B (he had a hairstyle somewhat like Johnny Bravo), but Clem called him Johnny T—as in T-Rex, because his hands couldn't reach his wallet whenever it was time to pay.

When I eventually came to my senses and cut the guy loose, I decided the next guy I date will have a well-paying job—preferably more than I make. If that makes me a terrible feminist, then so be it.

Not sure a bartender's pay would cut it, not to mention the fact that I'm really not interested in a player. I need somebody settled, not somebody who has no intentions of settling down anytime soon. I also want somebody intelligent and with a good sense of humor. That's not an unreasonable list, is it?

Ben may not fit the list, but my date tonight does.

At least, on paper he does. James is an accountant, so I can check off "stable job". I know from my depressing struggle with math at school, he has to be fairly intelligent to work with numbers all day, so I can check that off too. He said in his profile he was looking for something serious. Check. As for the sense of humor, I guess I'll have to find out.

I spend a few minutes chatting with Ben about London and dismal British weather, because of course, you're not truly a Brit unless you talk about the weather.

We also talk a little about travel before he asks, "Are you waiting for some friends?"

"I'm waiting for a blind date."

Did that sound as pathetic as I think it did? I'm sure he just winced and for some reason, I'm suddenly a bit embarrassed about the whole debacle.

I blush.

"Yeah. Single, new to the city, and having a kind of mid-life crisis. That pretty much sums me up," I admit in a moment of transparency.

At that summation, he lets out a huff of laughter and shakes his head. "Mid-life crisis? You look twenty-five tops, not forty-five."

"I'm twenty-nine actually," I reply with a grin, when what I really want to do is lean over the bar and kiss him for not thinking I look like I'm knocking on thirty.

Maybe tonight won't be so bad.

CHAPTER THREE

"KATE Callahan? Sorry I'm late." I hear a voice behind me and spin around on my stool.

"Yes," I confirm. "James? Hi. Nice to meet you," I say, reaching out to shake the hand of my blind date, who's twenty minutes late. I'm normally a stickler for time, but I've been enjoying Ben's company so much I hadn't even noticed.

Although his profile said he was thirty, James has a rapidly receding hairline and old-fashioned glasses that make him look older than he really is. His profile picture was obviously taken when he had a lot more hair.

He's wearing a grey suit, which seems a bit formal for a place like The Old Copper Pig. Although you can't see much of his skin, except what's above his collar, I'm struck by how pale he is, and coming from somebody English, that's saying something. Does this man ever see the sun?

As I withdraw my hand from an exceedingly limp handshake, James reaches into his pocket, pulls out a little bottle, and squirts something into his hand.

Did he just sanitize his hands?

I feel like I've suddenly been transported back to the days of Covid and facemasks.

I grab my wine glass and give Ben a quick smile, but he's not looking at me. He's looking at James, with a puzzled frown firmly etched on his handsome face. I can't help but wonder if that look is because he's wondering about my taste in men.

I try not to let my own disappointment register on my face as James leads us to our table. I knew going into this that I'd need to keep an open mind.

My astonishment only increases when we reach our table and James suddenly whips out a sanitizing wipe and wipes down his chair before sitting. Once seated, he takes out another wipe, and wipes the table in front of him. I wonder if he was like this before Covid. The way he seems reluctant to touch anything suggests he probably was, and is not the type to pull out chairs or open doors for ladies because that would mean touching things.

As we peruse the menu in awkward silence I can feel the panic starting to well up in me, but I try my best to squash it down. He may not be the type I normally go for, and he may be a bit of a germaphobe, but I hardly know the chap and I should really give him a chance. Perhaps he has a wonderful sense of humor.

After that little mental pep talk, the waiter comes to take our order. Before I can even open my mouth James launches into his order.

"I'll have the Asian-style honey chicken, but it can't be made with sesame oil and no sesame seeds. I'm allergic. With baby potatoes, but make sure the potatoes and chicken don't touch. And I'll have the salad on the side with dressing. Wait. Does the dressing have egg? I can't have egg. And sparkling water. In the bottle. You got that? Maybe you should be writing this down." He sounds annoyed already. "Service people these days," he mutters to himself, but loudly enough that both the server and I can hear.

I give an apologetic smile to the waiter and order the Friday night special, which is grilled cod with salsa rossa. My mum always used to tell me that the way a person treats *the help* tells you a lot about their character. She also told me never to be rude to a waiter because they may spit on your food. While the second tidbit may stem from her penchant for a bit of drama, it's good advice.

The waiter collects our menus and scampers away—probably trying to escape before James issues any more instructions.

James turns his gaze to me but doesn't say anything. He just stares. Not wanting to endure another minute of this uncomfortable silence, I try to initiate some conversation.

"So, James, tell me about your work. Your profile said you're an accountant?"

"Yes, at Johnston West. Typical nine-to-five desk job. Some people would say it's boring, but I love what I do." He pushes his glasses further up his nose with his bony index finger and I notice how fragile looking his pale hands are. "There's something about numbers that really speaks to me. What about you? Your profile said you're in public relations. What does that involve?"

His monotone delivery seems to suit his personality. At least he's asking questions.

"Our clients are mainly celebrities, so it sometimes involves crisis management when they've been getting up to mischief. Sometimes we're looking for opportunities to salvage reputations through media exposure and interviews. We arrange things like public appearances for fundraising, and write press releases. There's even some hobnobbing with the rich and famous. I also love what I do."

It's true. I really enjoy my work. In spite of my social ineptitude outside of work, I somehow manage just fine in my job. Probably because the slightly neurotic, control-freak part of me knows how to do things efficiently. Unlike dating, I know what I'm doing at my job and I'm good at it.

"Hobnobbing?"

"Yes. You know…socializing, like at charity events." Do they not use that word in America?

"Hmm." James flicks a glance at my folded hands that are resting on the table. I can see the wheels turning, but I have no idea what he's thinking. He clears his throat. "Does that mean you shake a lot of hands in your line of work?"

His left eye is starting to twitch.

"Yes, I guess so," I answer honestly. What a strange question.

I've barely got the words out of my mouth and he's taking out his hand sanitizer again with what can only be described as a look of revulsion aimed directly at my folded hands. He has no shame. This is more than just being cautious.

Once again, we fall into a painful silence and I realize this is going to be a long evening.

The waiter interrupts our awkward, stilted conversation as he sets our plates down in front of us. I'm impressed and rather grateful that our food came so quickly because I don't want this date to last a minute longer than necessary.

The food smells divine. I load a forkful of cod and salsa and bring it up to my mouth ready to savor the deliciousness before I hear James addressing the waiter again, which stops me in my tracks and leaves my fork suspended in mid-air.

"I can't eat this potato."

He stabs a finger towards the lone little potato that has wandered away from its friends and is just barely touching a piece of scrumptious looking honey chicken.

"They've touched," he explains, as if it should be obvious to the waiter why he can't eat it. "I can't eat this potato now." He shakes his head vigorously.

I'd make a terrible waitress because my mouth is still hanging open, and this time it's not because it's waiting for a forkful of food. I'm stunned at the tediousness of this man.

Unlike me, the very professional waiter doesn't blink. He simply apologizes, takes a fork out of his apron, and very carefully removes the offending potato without disturbing the rest of the food on the plate.

"Will that be satisfactory sir, or would you like me to get you a new meal?"

"I suppose this is fine," James says with a sigh as he begins wiping down his knife and fork with another sanitizing wipe.

I'm mentally calculating how much he must spend on those each month. One of the things I liked about his profile was his job because it fits *the list*. I thought an accountant at such a prestigious company must be ambitious and stable, but now I'm rethinking that. It's no wonder he has such a cushy job—he needs that big fat paycheck to pay for all his sanitizing wipes.

I sneak a glance over at Ben who's also watching the scene with his mouth hanging slightly open and one eyebrow sitting high up on his forehead. I'm glad I'm not the only one who thinks this is abnormal.

I want to ask why on earth it matters if the potatoes and chicken touch when they're all going to end up in the same place anyway, but I bite my tongue and concentrate on enjoying the delicious flavor of my grilled cod.

By the end of the main course, I'm convinced that James is definitely not my type, and I certainly won't be seeing him again. Okay, I confess I had already decided that about five minutes after meeting him, but the conversation over dinner has only reinforced that opinion.

He has a list of allergies as long as my arm and a color-coded wardrobe in various shades of gray and beige. Not that I'm against color-coding a wardrobe, because if I had more time to organize, I'd probably do that myself. The perfectionist in me appreciates that. It's just that it's a little unusual for a very drab-looking guy like James, and when you combine that with the fact that he looks so fragile he might blow over in a stiff breeze…well, he's just not my type.

I'm also not so sure about his allergies. How can one person be allergic to so many things? I'm surprised he managed to find anything on the menu that he could actually eat. Going by his aversion to germs, he's also a hypochondriac.

He's also very dull, like his gray and beige wardrobe, because no matter what question I ask him, and I've asked dozens, he always seems to somehow bring the conversation back around to his job or his allergies.

We're discussing dessert options when a man who has been smoking outside walks past my chair. The thick stench of cigarette smoke clings to his clothes and tickles my nose.

I know what's coming.

Ever since I was a child, the smell of smoke would make me sneeze. I quickly remove the napkin from my lap and turn to the side as I sneeze into it.

I wish I could say it was a polite, lady-like sneeze but it's more on the convulsing-banshee end of the spectrum. Thank goodness for the large napkin.

Sneezing discreetly has never been my strong suit, much to Mum's embarrassment. She cringes every time I sneeze, ever since the Remembrance Day incident. I was ten and sneezed repeatedly and violently during a moment of silence for fallen soldiers. My very prim and proper mum was mortified. It wasn't my fault smoky old Mr. Armstrong was sitting right in front of us.

Blowing my nose is not much better either. She banned me from blowing my nose in public, saying "Catherine, with that trumpeting, people will think you're ushering in the Second Coming," which is probably not too far from the truth, to be fair.

I blame my nan for this. I got my loud sneezing genes from her. When she was seventy, she got a hernia just below her sternum from sneezing so violently. It just popped up like a third boob! And we've lost count of the number of times her dentures have gone flying.

Looking up after my fierce episode, I register the absolute horror on James' face. If I thought I was bad at hiding my shock, James is ten times worse. He has reared back in his chair and is looking at me like I sneezed all over him and still have snot hanging out my nose. I self-consciously give my nose an extra wipe just in case I left any nasal ornaments.

Before I can properly process what's happening, James stands up, drops a wad of cash on the table, and says, "I'm sorry. You're very sweet, but I…I should have known this is just not going to work."

As he rushes out of the restaurant, I see him reach into his pocket for his little bottle of hand sanitizer.

I'm left sitting here, absolutely stunned.

Did that really just happen?

A voice echoes my thoughts. "Wow, did that really just happen?"

Turning my head, I see Ben standing next to the table, his eyes darting between me and the door. He looks halfway between amused and shocked.

I let out a huff of laughter. "Well, that didn't really go as planned."

"I can't say I've ever heard of a date running away because of a sneeze. Although, I've never heard a sneeze quite like that either," Ben teases.

I cover my face with my hands.

"I know! It's like a high-yield bomb exploding. I've tried to learn to do it more quietly. I really have!"

"Just don't go anywhere near small children…or really old people. Don't want to scare anybody to death."

I can't help but laugh at his teasing. Ben looks me directly in the eyes and it's a little bit unnerving. I feel…exposed, somehow. Like he can see right inside me.

"I hope you're not going to let him ruin your evening. Stay for dessert. We have an amazing selection."

"And sit here eating on my own after my date walked out on me? I already feel like a loser."

I look around to see if anybody has witnessed my humiliation, but nobody is paying any attention.

"Firstly, you're not on your own, I'm here," he replies as he takes James' vacated seat opposite me. "And secondly, if anybody is a loser, it's that guy. I've spoken to you for five minutes and already I know that you're funny, you're smart, and you're beautiful. It's definitely his loss," he says with a semblance of a smile that makes him look shy.

The sweet remark settles over me like a warm blanket.

"Thank you. I think that's the nicest thing anybody's ever said to me." I glance around the room. "Aren't you going to get in trouble for slacking on your shift? Or does the boss pay you to cheer up customers too?"

I don't know why my question amuses him so much but his hearty laugh cheers me up even more.

"Don't worry about my job. The boss is amazing. So, what's it gonna be? Lemon soufflé? Irish whisky truffles? A fudge sundae?"

"I think I'll leave the truffles and sundae for another day. I might pop if I have anything too rich," I say, rubbing my already full stomach. "The lemon soufflé sounds just right. Thank you."

He relays the order to the waiter who's back with the dessert in record time.

Two hours later I feel like Ben is already an old friend. We've talked about anything and everything. He told me about his parents moving to America from Ireland when he was just a baby and how he and his two younger brothers spent their childhood on the Vineyard giving their poor mammy Walsh gray hairs. I told him about my childhood in England, how I ended up in Boston, my desire to finally settle down, and how Clementine talked me into internet dating. I also told him about temporarily living with Dan and Clem and their delightful but very active twins, who are also prematurely aging my cousin with all their antics. They probably got those genes from my nan too. She's a feisty old lady. I don't remember laughing this much in a long time.

Glancing at my watch, I see that it's already almost eleven o'clock. I'm surprised that Clem hasn't phoned to check that I'm still alive.

"Wow. It's late. I'm going to get you fired."

I look around to see if there is anybody giving him the evil eye, but nobody seems to be paying any attention to us. He's probably going to get an earful from irate co-workers later. Thankfully the bar is not too busy so the other bartender seems to be managing fine on his own.

"I really should get going," I say as I stand and gather my purse. "Thank you for keeping me company. You really didn't have to. You turned what could have been an utter disaster into a wonderful evening."

Ben gently grabs my elbow and steers me toward the exit.

"Kate Callahan, the pleasure was all mine," he says as we reach the door.

He turns towards me, his warm hand still lightly holding my elbow. It still feels like he's looking right into me with those piercing eyes.

It's making me feel all warm and fuzzy, and a little bit uncomfortable because it's rather unexpected. We've only had one conversation; two, if you count the conversation we had at the bar when I arrived. And yet, it feels like he's an old friend. I haven't ever felt this connected to anybody I've only just met.

I don't want to become attached. I have to keep reminding myself that he's a bartender, who is most likely a player, and I need somebody who can offer the stability I want. No matter how much I might like him, he doesn't fit the list.

Ben looks like he wants to say something. Dragging his eyes away from my face, he chews on his bottom lip.

Just when I think he's going to stay silent he says, "Just…just promise me that the next blind date you have, you'll have here. I want you to be safe."

Like a love-struck teenager, I just nod. The gorgeous décor and scrumptious food would have been enough to make me come back anyway, but I don't tell him that.

He leans forward and gives me a soft peck on my cheek, his lips brushing lightly over my blushing skin. It's a whisper of a kiss, but it's enough to send my pulse racing.

In spite of my mind shouting instructions to hang tough, I can't help but lean into it just a tad. There's clearly a disconnect between my heart and my brain.

He smells like soap and leather, and I could stay in this moment forever.

CHAPTER FOUR

"SO, DID you do anything interesting this weekend darling?"

It's my usual Sunday phone call with Mum and I decide to drop the bomb.

"Actually Mum, I went on a blind date with a guy I met online," I say and wait for the explosion on the other end of the line.

I don't know why I provoke her like this. It's just so easy to get a reaction out of my dear mum. Although to be fair, I also had thoughts of serial killers and chopped-up bodies going through my head.

"Pardon?" I hear a rustle and can picture her suddenly sitting ramrod straight in her favorite chair, one hand on the phone in a white-knuckle grip and the other clutching the pearls at her neck.

I'm regretting not making this a video call but we tried that the first week I was in America. I spent the entire call looking just at Mum's chin. Technology is not her friend.

"Kate, you had better be joking. This is not funny…Harold! Harold!"

Luckily for my ears, she had pulled the phone away from her mouth before shrieking for my father.

"Catherine Louise Callahan, tell me you are joking! Do you have any idea how dangerous that is? How can you be so reckless? I…"

Uh oh, she used my full name. I'm in serious trouble now.

I interrupt her. "But you said you wanted me to settle down. I'm just taking *your* advice. I'm meeting new people through internet dating."

I grin, even though I know I'm just poking the bear.

"I never told you to go online dating!" she splutters. "I meant meet somebody at work, or through friends, or a nice young man at church, not somebody from the interweb! Oh darling, how do you know you're not meeting up with a serial killer, or a rapist?" She starts to hyperventilate. "I can't believe…Harold, do you know what your daughter has done?"

Dad has obviously come to find out what Mum is screeching about.

"She's finding dates on the interweb! I've read all about it, Harold. You don't know what kind of sick people are out there. Blind dates, Harold! Talk some sense into your daughter."

I hear a shuffle on the other end before I hear: "Hello darling," as Dad's comforting baritone voice rumbles down the line.

"Hello, Dad."

"So, blind dates, eh? Sounds like an adventure."

I can't help but laugh because I can hear my mum in the background. She is not pleased with Dad. Not pleased at all.

"Well, the first one was certainly an adventure. He was a germaphobe accountant who walked out on me before we even got to dessert."

"Oh dear." Dad chuckles. I can just picture him resting his hand on his big belly as it bounces up and down.

"Yes. He left as soon as I sneezed."

Dad's chuckle turns into a full belly laugh.

"Yes, well that would do it, now wouldn't it? I hope he at least paid for your meal sweetheart."

Dear, old-fashioned Dad is a firm believer in men being gentlemen—opening doors for their lady, pulling out chairs, and paying for the meal.

"You know these days it's normal to split the bill, Dad. But yes, he left a wad of cash on the table before he walked out on me. I've got another date lined up for Friday."

"Good. You must find somebody who treats you right. I don't want to have to take out my gun."

I roll my eyes. "You don't even own a gun, Dad."

My father is a teddy bear who wouldn't hurt a fly.

"Have fun on your blind dates darling, but do be sensible.

Otherwise I'm going to be in trouble with the boss," he says with a chuckle.

Dad loves referring to Mum as the boss, but he's not really a pushover. In fact, he's probably the only man on earth who knows just how to handle her. He has the patience of a saint.

"I will, Dad. I'm always careful. Does Mum want to talk again?"

"She left the room in a huff when I didn't do as I was told," he replies, sounding as cheeky as I am when I try to get a rise out of her. "Never mind your mum. She'll get over it. I love you, sweetheart. Stay safe."

"I love you too, Dad."

***

Monday morning starts off with a bang because I'm running late and did I mention I hate being late? I was raised better than that. In Felicity Callahan's book of manners, being late is the height of rudeness.

I rush through the revolving doors of our building which sits in the middle of the bustling financial district. I'm only ten minutes late.

Thankfully the boss is nowhere in sight as I drop into my chair and unpack my laptop. Mr. Turner is a stickler for rules and time management. He'd get on fabulously with Mum. I should introduce them. On second thought, Mum would love him so much she'd probably play matchmaker and I have no desire to marry an uptight man who is at least thirty years older than me. I'll nix that plan.

I'm just tucking away my laptop bag when a head pops over the partition that separates my cubicle from the one to the right of me. It's my French neighbor Alex.

Being the headquarters of an international company, it's really a mixed bag here. On my first day, when he found out I was English, he went and labeled our shared partition The English Channel. And by that, I mean he printed out a label and physically put it on the partition.

He is funny, and flamboyant, and just one of the reasons I love my new job, although I would never tell him that because his little French head would swell to epic proportions.

"So…'ow was the blind date? We want all the juicy details."

I roll my eyes at Alex who is dressed in a very bright turquoise shirt and is practically vibrating with excitement. He looks like a kid on Christmas morning.

It took me just one day working in this office to realize that if you want any office gossip, celebrity gossip, or really *any* gossip, Alex is your man. He knows everything about everyone and is usually more than willing to share this wealth of knowledge. But everything sounds better in a strong French accent so you can't dislike him.

Just like I do with my mother, I can't resist teasing him a bit. I give him one word.

"Disaster."

"No!" He puts his hand on his chest. "But why?…'er date was a disaster!"

I spin in my chair to see who he is talking to and see Viola standing behind me.

When I grow up, I want to be Viola. She is beautiful, as in drop-dead-gorgeous-could-easily-be-a-model beautiful. She's tall and graceful, and could make even a brown paper bag look stylish if she wore it. She's also funny, and the kindest, sweetest person you'll ever meet…unless she's dealing with Noah King. The famous Formula 1 driver is her biggest client and also the biggest pain in her backside. I'm not sure what it is about him, but he pushes every button she has.

"Oh dear. Wasn't what you expected?" she asks as she drops her bag on her desk which is located directly opposite mine. Apparently, I'm not the only one running late today.

"No. He was a balding germaphobe who walked out on me."

I end up sharing the whole story, in detail, because Alex won't let me start working until I've given him a play-by-play of exactly what went down. I even share the bit about gorgeous bartender Ben. Alex's eyes dance with excitement. No doubt he's storing away the details to repeat at a later stage.

***

The rest of the week is spent doing damage control for a couple of my A-list clients who got up to mischief over the weekend, as well as formulating a PR strategy for an up-and-coming singer who is a new client. Usually I thrive on the challenge, but today I can't concentrate the way I normally do. That's probably because a certain blue-eyed bartender is constantly popping up in my thoughts.

Shoving my laptop back into its bag, I try to simultaneously shove aside any thoughts of Ben, but it's proving particularly difficult today because it's Friday and I have another blind date at The Old Copper Pig. Knowing that I'll see Ben again tonight gives me a thrill that zings through my body in a most unwelcome way.

I don't want to think about him this way because as gorgeous as he is, he can't give me what I need in a relationship right now. I mentally run through my checklist, reminding myself why dating him would be a terrible idea.

I'm just standing up to leave when Viola comes storming out of the conference room with her fists clenched at her sides. Even when she's mad, she looks graceful. Noah King is walking with his hands in his pockets at a leisurely pace behind her, without a care in the world. At his height, his long legs eat up the space between them and even at his leisurely pace, he has no trouble keeping up with her angry steps.

"It's not a big deal. I don't know why you're getting so worked up about it."

At the sound of Noah's voice, Alex's head pops up to look over the partition. He reminds me of a meerkat.

He's just in time to see Viola spin around on her high heels and glare at Noah while she rubs her temples, as if she's trying to massage away a headache.

"Not a big deal? Not a big deal?" She enunciates each word slowly and if I looked really closely, I'm sure I'd actually be able to see steam coming out of her ears.

You'd be forgiven for thinking that Noah's trouble is of the female variety, because honestly, a large portion of the damage control we do for our celebrity clients is because of some *indiscreet* moments. Especially clients as handsome and as famous as Noah King. The ladies are *wild* about the guy.

Well, in this case, you'd be wrong. I don't think Noah has ever even been photographed with a woman. The gorgeous caveman probably hasn't even had a girlfriend.

His problems are more of the flipped-the-press-off variety. He is a grump through and through. He doesn't like anybody and getting him to do anything is like trying to draw blood from a stone. Good luck with that. The complete opposite of our ray of sunshine, Viola.

"You've just undone all my hard work you big buffoon! Do you have any idea of the fire that I'm left to put out? I'll answer that for you: no, because you're a selfish jackass!"

I press my lips together to suppress a laugh. I don't know of any other publicist who calls their paying client a big buffoon and jackass, but Noah doesn't care. Truly.

He just shrugs and says, "That's why I pay you," as he walks out of the office with a swagger that leaves all the females in the vicinity drooling.

The first time Viola called Noah a jackass, the big boss overheard. Old Mr. T, shocked at the uncharacteristic outburst from delightful, sweet-natured Viola, told her in no uncertain terms that he was pulling her from that account immediately. He also told her that if Noah complained about her behavior, she was going to be fired.

But neither of those things happened. In fact, not only did Noah *not* complain, but he refused to let anybody else handle his PR when Turner apologized and tried to assign a new publicist. Noah threatened to take his business elsewhere if Viola was removed from his account. He only wants Viola.

I wasn't around for that particular show, but I've heard a very detailed report from Alex. The funny thing is that Viola really is the sweetest person. She is a complete professional and a delight to most of her clients. Just not Noah.

As for Noah, he just grunts and shrugs most of the time (which is part of what makes Viola's job so hard). Actually, the conversation today is probably the most I've ever heard him talk in one go. He's probably used up his entire quota of words for the day. Poor Viola.

Well, at least that was an entertaining way to end the week.

CHAPTER FIVE

I HEAVE a sigh of relief as I head towards my date for tonight, who's already seated at a table and was easy to spot because, unlike the first guy, this guy looks exactly like his profile picture.

On the way, I sneak a glance towards the bar where Ben is chatting to a customer. A female customer who looks like she's really turning on the charm by the way she's giggling. She looks like Barbie.

Even though I realize I have absolutely no claim on him, it doesn't stop me from wanting to march over there and rip her hand away when she touches his arm playfully.

Ben only smiles politely as he steps out of her reach. Although she looks like she wouldn't turn down a roll in the hay with him, he definitely looks disinterested. That shouldn't make me happy, but it does. I've only met the guy once! I'm sure this is not a healthy response.

He sees me walking past and gives me a quick wink which makes my heart flutter a little. I'd better get that under control. Especially because it's not very fair on my actual date for the night.

"You must be Kate. Hi, I'm Oliver."

Before I can stretch my hand out, Oliver leans over, takes a hold of my upper arm and gives me a quick peck on the cheek. The greeting reminds me of a summer I spent in France where everybody and their uncle kisses your cheeks. Perhaps Oliver has some French blood in him. Alex would be thrilled. It's a bit unexpected and forward from an American, but with the adorable grin on his face I can't really be too upset about it.

"You're just as beautiful as your photo–which is quite a relief after some of the dates I've been on." He chuckles. "I've been looking forward to this all week. Wanna share a starter?"

He's cute and funny and the conversation flows easily over dinner, the only problem is that he keeps mentioning his ex. I probably know more about his ex-girlfriend than I do about him: her name is Tiffany, she works for a high-profile fashion magazine, she's a vegan, she has three cats. This is not going to work—he clearly isn't over her, poor chap.

I lean towards him and lower my voice slightly.

"Oliver, I don't really know how to say this without being rude, so I'm just going to come right out and say it. Are you sure you're over Tiffany?" I ask in the gentlest way possible. "She's all you talk about. Are you sure that chapter is really closed?"

He shifts in his seat.

"Of course. Yes. For sure. Definitely." He doesn't sound offended. With the number of synonyms he's throwing out, it sounds more like he's trying to convince himself.

"If you don't mind me asking, how did things end?"

"We ended things six months ago although we still talk almost every day. It was all very amicable. Our schedules just didn't work. She works long hours and helps with the magazine's photoshoots so she often travels to exotic locations. She could've been a model herself. Legs for days. Here, I'll show you."

With that proclamation, he takes out his wallet and extracts a photo of Tiffany and holds it under my nose. Not even a photo on his phone, an actual printed photo. It's very…old-school.

I open and close my mouth several times. He's going to think I'm a fish, but I have no idea what to say. I'm speechless. Six months after a break-up he still carries a photo of his ex with him wherever he goes? And he still talks to her every day? Is that normal?

The worn edges of the photo show just how many times he's fished it out to look at it. If he has a printed photo, I'd hate to think of how many photos of her he still has on his phone. From the way he talks about her, he probably has multiple albums dedicated to her.

However, shocked or not, my curiosity can't be ignored and I take a look at the photo. I can see what he means. She's tall, has high cheekbones, and is built for the runway.

"She's lovely." Although a bit on the thin side…not that I say that out loud.

Instead, I ask, "Do, uh, all your ex-girlfriends look like this?"

I'm trying to work out why on earth he even clicked on my profile if this is the sort of body type he normally goes for. I will never look like that. I'm not overweight, by any means. I work out regularly to keep trim, but I like steak and pizza and cheeseburgers way too much to ever look like that. This poor girl looks like she's never seen a cheeseburger in her life. I can see her ribs poking out thanks to her bikini, which doesn't leave much to the imagination.

"Yes, but don't worry. I don't mind dating somebody a bit more bulky, you know."

A bit more bulky? Excuse me? How rude!

I glance over at Ben and can't help but think I'd much rather be sitting chatting with him than hearing all about Oliver's ex.

"It's a really pretty beach." I hand the photo back and try to steer the conversation in a different direction.

"Oh yeah, it was in Thailand. She said it was amazing. Here, I'll show you."

He pulls out his phone and opens an album before handing it over. My suspicions are confirmed. The album is filled with dozens and dozens of photos of her in Thailand. Some on the beautiful beaches, some in rural-looking villages, some in Bangkok. She is in every shot. She may not be a model, but she certainly knows how to pose like one. She must have been taking notes during the magazine photoshoots.

"It's lovely," I say, handing the phone back.

"She also went on a magazine shoot in Japan. You should see the scenery there! It was cherry blossom season. I can show you."

He's about to swipe to another album when I say, "No, really, don't worry about it. Thanks."

It comes out a bit strangely. I hope he doesn't think I'm being rude but what else am I supposed to do? I don't want to spend the entire date scrolling through photos of the guy's ex-girlfriend.

He seems to get the hint because the rest of the meal is pleasant enough and I find out a little bit more about Oliver as we chat about our hobbies and work. I appreciate the fact that he's clearly making an effort not to mention his ex again. However, the damage is done and I decline dessert because I know I won't be seeing Oliver again.

There's no point in dragging this out longer. It doesn't matter if he seems like a good guy, I don't want to be competing with an ex that he is very clearly not over.

We get up and make our way toward the door of The Old Copper Pig.

"I really enjoyed this evening, Kate. I hope we can do it again. I'll call you."

Oliver leans over and kisses my cheek before he disappears out the door and into the crowds who are enjoying an evening out on this trendy street.

Hearing him say he'll call makes me regret giving him my phone number, but it's far easier to arrange dates that way instead of messaging back and forth online. I don't think crusty old Mr. Turner would appreciate me spending all my time at work on a dating website.

I smile at the thought as I place my hand on the door, getting ready to exit myself, but before I get anywhere, I hear somebody calling my name.

"Kate!"

I spin around and see Ben behind the bar. Giggling Barbie is still there giving Ben flirty doe-eyes and doesn't look too thrilled that he called my name.

Ben inclines his head, motioning for me to come over. I happily oblige and plonk myself down on a stool in front of him while he wipes down the countertop. Aside from me and the blonde, this side of the long bar is quiet.

"Are you going to introduce your friend, Ben?"

The slight emphasis she puts on the word *friend* doesn't go unnoticed. Judging by the smirk on Ben's face, he noticed it too.

"Kate this is Courtney. Courtney, Kate."

I don't know what to make of the fact that they seem to know each other fairly well. Well enough that she's asking him to introduce us and seems to be a bit…territorial about him. It's just a vibe I get from her. Although it's a bit rich coming from me, considering how territorial I was feeling about him earlier. Pot, kettle, and all that.

I don't want to dwell on it though, because, as I reminded myself earlier, I have no claim on him. We had one long, really lovely conversation last week, but I hardly know the guy.

Barbie…uh, Courtney, gives me a very insincere smile but perks up a little bit when Ben asks, "So, how was the second blind date?"

"You were on a blind date? Oh, bless your heart. How

very…desperate."

Ouch. She laughs and it sounds about as genuine as her red, talon-like nails and bleached blonde hair.

I ignore Courtney's little jab and look at Ben who's completely focused on me and biting on his bottom lip. It's a nervous gesture but it seems out of place. Ben definitely strikes me as the calm, self-confident type.

I sigh.

"That bad?" he asks with a cheeky grin and a twinkle in his eye.

I smile back because I just can't help myself.

"No, not really. He actually seems like a good guy but he talked non-stop about his ex for most of the date. I even got to see a photo of her that he fished out of his wallet, and an entire album of her on his phone."

"He keeps an actual photo of his ex with him?" His one eyebrow is almost touching his hairline and I'm glad I'm not the only one who thinks that's definitely out of the ordinary.

"I know! And the album I looked at on his phone wasn't the only one full of her photos. And they still talk every day. That's not normal, is it? She looks like a model. And what's worse is that he called me *bulky! Bulky!*"

At that little tidbit of information, Ben laughs a full belly laugh. I can't tell if he's laughing because he also thinks that's absurd or because of the disgusted expression on my face.

Courtney joins in. This time, her laugh sounds completely genuine. She's probably delighted at the thought of me as *bulky*.

Ben presses his lips together and gets his laugh under control just as Courtney weighs in on the comment.

"You can't really blame him now can you? I mean, he dated a *model* before you, and you're…well, you're no model, that's for sure."

The audacity! Oh, I *really* don't like Courtney.

I'm so astonished by how rude she is that I don't bother to correct her. Tiffany worked for a magazine; she wasn't a model…even if she did look like one.

Ben seems to be completely ignoring Courtney. With his eyes fixed on me, he pats my hands which are folded in front of me and says, "You're perfect. Stay for a drink?"

Well, now he's just got my head in a muddle.

I'm flattered that he called me perfect and wants me to stay for a drink, but the way he patted my hand? That was a "there-there" friend gesture if ever I saw one. Although, I'm not sure how Courtney interpreted it, because she looked momentarily stricken.

I shouldn't feel so disappointed that Ben isn't interested in me, because I've already established that he's not looking for anything serious, and he's a bartender at that. No matter what the little flutter in my belly tells me, he's off-limits. Although I could use a friend outside of work.

I glance at my watch and see that it's still early. "Sure, why not?"

Barbie clearly doesn't like this little interaction between us because she interrupts our conversation with a little pout. She tries to lean over the bar and attempts to stroke Ben's arm, but he smoothly moves it out of the way before she can make contact.

"So Benny Boo, when are we going out again? You know how much fun we had last time."

She gives him a wink that makes me want to gag.

Ugh. Really? They've been on a date? I just can't see it, but if this really is the kind of woman Ben goes for, then he's definitely not my type. There is nothing about her that seems genuine and I'm not just talking about her appearance.

"I already told you Courtney, I'm not interested in going out with you."

"Aw don't be coy now, big boy."

This time I really do have to stop myself from gagging. *Big boy?* Somebody pass the sick bucket!

She turns to me and lowers her voice, although it's still loud enough for Ben to hear. I think she's aiming for a sultry whisper but it comes out more like smoky old Mr. Armstrong's croak.

"We had an amaaazing time. He's so delicious, you have no idea…" She trails off as she licks her plump red lips and I have to make a concerted effort to school my expression into something neutral to hide the absolute distaste I feel at this information.

Ben flings the cloth that was over his shoulder onto the counter with a *thwack* that makes both of us jump.

"Courtney, I'm not sure how many times and in how many ways I have to say this: I'm not interested in dating you. I apologize if that hurts your feelings, but I'm not going to change my mind."

This is the first time I've seen Ben look irritated. He normally comes across as really relaxed.

Courtney huffs in frustration.

"You're going to regret this Ben. And when you come crawling back to me, I might just be unavailable. I'm a catch, you know?"

She flicks her blonde hair over her shoulder and I watch as she struts out of the bar with a little swing to her hips.

I turn back to Ben with an eyebrow raised. I don't even have to say anything. He knows exactly what I'm thinking.

"It's not what it looks like." He rolls his eyes. "Same as last time?"

As much as I want to be honest about the wine, it's just so embarrassing coming clean. I can't have him giving it to me every time I come because he thinks that's what I like, but how do I explain that asking for wine that first night was because of a brain-to-mouth malfunction? Blasted social anxiety! I decide to keep it simple.

"The wine was nice, but I'll just have a Coke, thanks."

"Just a soda?" Curiosity is etched on his face when I nod, but he doesn't say anything more and, coward that I am, I don't enlighten him as he pours me the drink. When I try to slide some cash towards him he just shakes his head. I guess this is on the house.

"So…it's not what it looks like, huh?"

I may hardly know the guy, but I'm too curious not to ask what that little scene was all about. Alex would be proud. Thankfully, Ben doesn't disappoint.

He shakes his head and lets out a tired sigh.

"Definitely not! My parents know her parents. About a month ago my mom called and asked if I'd show her around the city a bit because she'd just moved to Boston from the South. I was happy to help. I spent the day taking her on the Freedom Trail. I made the mistake of ending the day with dinner."

"Ah. And she thought it was a date?"

"Yes!" He looks horrified by the thought. "She'd been fine all day, aside from a flirty comment now and then, but suddenly at dinner she was all over me. She pulled her chair around to my side of the table and kept touching me. It was like being smothered by a love-starved panda. I had to keep pushing her hands off me!"

I shouldn't laugh, but the disgusted expression on his face makes it hard to contain. I can just picture the scene.

"Oh goodness! She tried to snog you, didn't she?"

"Please don't remind me! It was traumatic. I had to lean so far back I was practically touching the neighboring table. Just trying to keep her hands off me was hard enough. She has more hands than an octopus has tentacles. They were everywhere. It was like trying to play whack-a-mole. I'd just push one away, and another one would pop up somewhere."

Now I really can't contain my laughter.

"Oh dear. And now she's stalking you?"

"Yeah, she comes to the bar every few days and I just can't seem to shake her. I've told her again and again that I'm not interested in her but she has the persistence of a telemarketer…and the subtlety of a jackhammer. Thank heavens I didn't tell her where I lived!"

He suppresses a shudder at the thought, which just makes me laugh more.

"So…any more blind dates lined up for this weekend?" He's not looking at me when he casually changes the subject. Instead, he busies himself with packing away glasses under the counter.

"No, I thought I'd better spend the weekend seeing some of the sights while I'm here. You know, immerse myself in the culture and all that."

"While you're here? Is the move only temporary?" Ben's back to chewing his lip. It must just be a habit.

"No, not at all. I love America and hopefully it won't be a problem to renew my work visa when it expires. I'll stay here as long as you guys will have me."

"Hmm, and how is that cultural immersion going so far?"

"Slowly. I haven't done much outside of work. Nothing really, aside from two blind dates." I must sound like an unsociable, terribly dull person.

"You've come to Red Sox territory in the middle of baseball season but you haven't been to a baseball game since you arrived?" He looks surprised.

"No. I'll get to one eventually."

"How about next weekend? There's a game on Saturday and I've got awesome tickets."

"Really? Wow."

I'm not sure if it's a good idea.

As easy as it is to talk to Ben, I don't want to get too attached to him. I'm pleased to know that Barbie isn't his type, but it doesn't change the fact that he still doesn't fit the list. But I also don't want to be a stick in the mud and spend all my weekends at home because I don't know anybody.

He taps my arm in a friendly gesture.

"Come on, it'll be fun. Didn't you say you still needed to make new friends in America?" he says, as if he can sense my hesitation.

And that seals the deal. I'll go. He may not be interested in a relationship, and his job may not fit the list, but I'm in a new country and I could always do with another friend.

Yes. That's what Ben and I will be. *Just friends.*

I nod, more to myself than to Ben, because I feel more settled about our budding friendship.

"Okay. Sounds good," I say as I down the last of the Coke.

"If you're free that morning, I can take you to some of the popular sights around the city too. They'll be packed full of tourists, but I promise you, it'll be worth it."

"Sure, why not?"

He gives me a Hollywood-worthy smile that makes me swoon on the inside, and before I know what's happening, he grabs my phone which was sitting on the bar top, punches his number in, and calls himself. The cheeky chap. I really need to put a lock on that thing.

"There. Now we have each other's numbers. I'll message you during the week to make plans."

He's looking very pleased with himself.

"I'm looking forward to it. I'd better get going," I say as I gather my purse.

I start heading for the door, before stopping and turning around again.

"Oh and Ben…I promise if we go to dinner afterwards, I won't cling to you like an octopus."

I give him a cheeky grin and as I turn back and head out the door, I can hear Ben's laughter behind me.

I hope the week goes quickly.

CHAPTER SIX

"SO, HOW did it go?"

Hearing my cousin's voice is the perfect way to brighten up a Monday morning. Dan and Clem were away the entire weekend. Seeing that Ben is taking me sightseeing on Saturday, I decided to have a quiet weekend at home reading. While I've loved having some peace and quiet at their place, I've been bursting at the seams to tell her about Friday night.

"Not great. I mean, Oliver was nice enough and he was pretty cute, but he talked about his ex-girlfriend most of the night."

There's a small gasp on the other end of the phone, just as Alex's head pops up from his side of the partition. I'm surprised he didn't ambush me as soon as I walked in this morning. For that small mercy, I have to thank one of Alex's celebrity clients, who was arrested this weekend trying to sneak his pet llama through airport security.

Alex is working overtime to create some kind of positive PR out of the whole debacle. Who buys a llama on vacation overseas, then brings it back on their private jet and tries to sneak it into the country? A deluded rapper, that's who. More money than sense. I have no idea how Alex is going to spin his client out of this one. This morning he asked me if there was such a thing as an "emotional support llama".

Right now, though, Alex seems to have redirected his attention from his clients' woes to my dating disasters. I should keep a diary just for him to rifle through. He'd love that.

"Really?" Clementine asks. "I thought that was rule number one for first dates: don't talk about your ex."

"Well, I guess Oliver didn't get the memo because I had to spend the whole night listening to how amazing Tiffany the vegan is." I try to ignore Alex, who is still unashamedly listening to my end of the conversation.

"Put it on speaker," he whispers as he motions with his hands.

And have the whole office hear? No, thank you. What a cheek! Besides, I know he has work to do. Instead of doing what he asks, I give Alex a dirty look and swivel on my chair so that my back is to him.

"…and he ended the evening by saying he wants to see me again."

"So, what are you going to do?"

"I'm about to send him a firm but polite message saying that I had a nice evening, that he's a great person who deserves somebody wonderful, it's just not me and I wish him all the best. Or something like that."

Clem laughs. "A termination message. I like it! You can copy and paste whenever you don't want to see a date again."

"I have to send it soon before he sends one trying to arrange another date."

The idea of it sends a wave of exhaustion through me. I can't take another evening of discussing Tiffany.

"I'd better let you get to it then…"

"No!" I practically shout down the line. "Wait, I didn't tell you what happened afterwards." I'm sure my cousin can hear the excitement in my voice. I need to tone it down.

I swivel back around and see that Alex is still listening intently to my side of the conversation. He's practically licking his lips in anticipation of what came next. Nosy parker.

"Well, spit it out then. What happened?" It seems Alex isn't the only one chomping at the bit to hear what happened.

I lower my voice slightly. "As I was about to walk out the door, bartender Ben stopped me and asked me how the date had gone, which didn't seem to impress the blonde bimbo at the bar that was all over him." I pause and wait for her reaction.

"Wait. He's dating somebody? Who is she? And *blonde bimbo*? It's not like you to be so critical of other women, Kate," she chides.

I feel just a teeny bit bad for being so judgemental. But not too bad. She was mean.

"Courtney, and he's not dating her. Don't feel too bad for her Clem. She called my attempt at internet dating desperate and said that I was no model."

There are titters from Alex.

"Ha! How rude! The blonde bimbo!" I can always count on Clementine to have my back.

"It was. She really wasn't nice. And very territorial. I think she was trying to stake her claim on Ben, but he was having none of it."

I tell Clem, and by extension Alex, all about Ben and Courtney's dinner that wasn't a date and how she's been practically stalking him since.

"She left in a bit of a huff. Ben and I chatted for a while after that. Anyway, the upshot is that we exchanged phone numbers because I'm going sightseeing and to a Red Sox game with him on Saturday."

Alex squeals and claps his hands together.

"Wow. Is it, like, a date? Does that mean the internet dating is on hold for a while?" Clem asks.

"No." I sigh. "His job doesn't really fit the list, and remember, he said on the first night I met him that he's not in a hurry to settle down. Then on Friday he patted my hand like I was a little kid. I think whatever attraction is there, it's definitely one-sided."

I can't hide the disappointment in my voice.

Clementine scoffs. "Bah, he must be blind then. You're a knock-out."

"Doesn't matter. Even if Ben was interested in me, he's said outright he's not looking for anything serious, and I'm not interested in being a notch on anybody's bedpost. We're not looking for the same thing, Clem. He doesn't fit the list. Besides, as Ben pointed out, I need to make new friends. So, I'm going to go to the game with my new *friend*. It'll be fun. Plus, I've already got the next date lined up for Thursday night."

"You and that blasted list. Okay, well—Stop licking the floor!"

I pull the phone away from my ear slightly. Dan and Clem have three-year-old twins. Boys. It wouldn't be a normal conversation with her if it wasn't punctuated with "Where are your pants?", "Stop trying to pee on the dog!" or "Don't eat the dog food" at least once.

"I've got to scram before the twins end up licking something even worse. See you later." She ends the call before I even get a chance to respond.

"Baseball game, *ma cherie*?" Alex looks skeptical and I can't tell if it's because he thinks I don't look like the type of girl who would enjoy baseball, or if it's the date-that's-not-a-real-date thing.

Ignoring him, I huff out a little sigh and quickly tap out my termination message to Oliver.

Before I can get much work done my phone pings with a message. I pick it up with a mixture of curiosity and trepidation. I hope Oliver took it well. To my complete surprise, the message is not from Oliver but from Ben.

Ben: Hope you enjoyed the rest of your w-end. We still on for Saturday? Text your address.

I can't help the grin on my face as I send him my address. He replies straight away.

Ben: Pick you up at 8am?

CHAPTER SEVEN

WALKING into the Old Copper Pig on Thursday night feels like coming home.

It looks small from the outside, but the interior stretches far back, and with the high ceilings it feels very spacious. The chatter of happy customers makes the atmosphere warm and homey. The inside is modern but still utterly charming.

Glancing towards the bar, I'm disappointed to see there's no Ben in sight. Maybe he has the night off.

I'm pleased that Hugh, my date for tonight, looks just like his profile picture. He's older than I normally go for and with less hair than I normally like. He's thirty-eight and shaved bald, but he's one of those guys who can pull it off, which is one of the reasons why I swiped right. And of course, the muscles bulging under his tight black shirt don't hurt either. He looks like he could bench press me without breaking a sweat.

Hugh rises from his chair and engulfs me in a warm hug when I reach the table. Yes, this guy definitely spends a lot of time in the gym. He's buff.

"I'm so happy to finally meet you, Kate." I think his face might split open he's grinning so wide, which makes me smile too.

We've been messaging each other for a couple of weeks now and have lots in common. Throughout our meal he has me belly-laughing with his great sense of humor. I think I may have even snorted once or twice. We both love reading, hiking, and traveling, which is probably why the conversation seems to flow so well. That is, until he gets all serious and starts a sentence with:

"Kate, there's something you need to know..."

My stomach drops. Experience has taught me that sentences that begin this way are never good.

"I'm serious about wanting a relationship that hopefully leads to marriage, but, um," he clears his throat, "I have a friend-with-benefits that I get together with every Wednesday night. Now, before you freak out thinking she has ulterior motives, you need to know that she's actually married to somebody else and isn't looking for anything more. It's an arrangement that I'm not willing to give up until the day I get married."

Oh good gracious!

I can't possibly have heard right. Ulterior motives weren't what first came to mind with this bombshell. I don't even know where to begin unpacking that statement. I decide to start with the "until the day I get married" part.

"I'm sorry, I'm not sure I understand. You're saying that, hypothetically, you would date me and maybe even get engaged at some point, but keep your friend-with-benefits until the day we got married?"

I know I sound a bit slow. I just can't help it. I'm in shock.

"Yes."

"Why? Why on earth would you do that? And she's married!"

That came out a bit more aggressively than intended, but I'm blaming the shock. He's already a write-off, but I'm desperate to understand how anybody would be okay with an arrangement like this.

Are they really just friends? What about her husband? She may want nothing more, but is Hugh secretly in love with her? I have so many questions rushing through my mind I can't even think straight.

"Look, I know it's not conventional." *He can say that again!* "It's just that I've known her for years. She's ten years older than me. She's settled and comfortable. We have a good arrangement that suits both of us. I don't want to mess that up in case things don't end up working out, you know?"

So, she's a bit of a cougar? I feel ill.

"But even when you're engaged?"

"Even an engagement isn't a sure thing. I've had a broken

engagement once before. Until I actually get my bride down the aisle, anything could happen."

Well, I'm not surprised he had a broken engagement if this is what was happening on the side.

"But why not just put things on pause while you wait to see if your new relationship works out? And why didn't you put that you're looking for an open relationship on your profile?"

I hope that didn't sound rude, but I'm still trying to figure out why he wasn't just transparent about this. If I'd had this information from the start, I never would have even considered going on a date with him.

"It's not an open relationship." He must notice my eyebrow lift skeptically because he plows on. "Don't think of it that way. Think of it more as a business relationship. There are no feelings involved, but she's a good friend who's a really important part of my life. I don't expect people to understand it, but it is what it is. But I'm serious about wanting to pursue a relationship with you."

He's clearly not budging. Not that it makes any difference to me—this is already a non-starter. I notice that he didn't answer the first question about why he doesn't just put it on hold, but it's pointless pushing him for an answer when it really won't change anything.

"I don't even know what to say to that." I shake my head from side to side as if that will somehow make me process this information better. "It's absolutely a no-go for me. I'm sorry. I mean, do you think you're going to find somebody who is okay with that? You say it's not an open relationship so does that mean they don't get to have a friend-with-benefits too? If you do eventually get married, will you stay friends with her? And what about her husband, does he even know?"

For somebody who doesn't know what to say, I sure find a lot to say. My rapid-fire questions don't seem to put Hugh off.

"Well, no." He frowns and shakes his head. "It's not an open relationship so I wouldn't want my partner to have an arrangement like that too. This is an exceptional circumstance. We've had this arrangement for almost ten years."

His hypocrisy is mindboggling. I'm struggling to grasp his logic. Ten years!

"And, yes, of course we'd stay friends. She's a huge part of my life. And yes, the husband knows." Hugh smiles mildly.

This is absolutely wild. I feel like I'm being punked and am just waiting for somebody to jump out with a camera. Who would want their partner to stay friends with an old friend-with-benefits?

"They have a somewhat unconventional marriage," he continues. "They live completely separate lives. She lives in an in-law suite on his property. It's all very amicable. The only reason they're not divorced is to do with finances."

"So, he's just okay with you hooking up with his wife every Wednesday?"

I can't believe people like this actually exist. I'll never understand how people can be completely happy with relationships like this. I like to think I'm a pretty secure person, but I'd never cope with a relationship like that. Have I lived such a sheltered life? Am I such a prude?

"He doesn't care. Really." Hugh obviously spots the dubious look I'm sending his way. "He doesn't even care that I'm taking her to Germany next month for a week."

"You're taking her to Germany?"

You couldn't shock me more if you hooked me up to a car battery with jumper cables.

"It's a business trip and she's tagging along. She likes German beer," he says with a shrug, as if it makes complete sense to take another man's wife on holiday.

"So, uh…hypothetically speaking, if we were to date and I couldn't go abroad with you because of work commitments, would you take her with instead?"

I don't know why I even bother asking these questions because I'd rather dodge a swarm of bees naked than be in a relationship with a guy like Hugh. Call it curiosity though. If nothing else, this information will be good fodder for Alex.

"Yes, probably. She also loves traveling. Look Kate, I really like you. You're gorgeous and funny. There's chemistry between us. I know you feel it too. I think we could be great together. Is there no way this is something you could work around?"

I hate how hopeful he sounds. It makes me laugh because really, that's the only response I can have to such ridiculousness.

"I'm sorry Hugh. You seem like a nice guy…" That's actually not an accurate statement at all. I mean, sure he's funny and easy going, but do nice guys sleep with other people's wives while they're dating somebody else? I think not, but it's not like I can say I suddenly think he's a horrible bloke. "…but there is just no way I would *ever* be okay with this. It's just not going to happen. I'm sorry."

I have to give the guy credit because instead of just ending the date, he brushes off my rejection and switches the conversation back to our mutual interests.

***

I let my head fall back on the headrest behind me and release a big sigh. Who would've thought it would be so hard to find just average, regular Joes in the online dating world?

I'm just about to start my car and head home when I hear the ping of a message on my phone.

BEN: So how was the date?
KATE: How did you know I was on a date?
BEN: I have my ~~spies~~ methods.
KATE: You're stalking me now?

The idea of Ben keeping tabs on me makes me grin to myself like a fool. If it was anybody else, I'd probably be freaking out, but this is Ben.

BEN: Maybe. So how was it?
KATE: Fine…until he said he planned to keep his Wednesday night friend-with-benefits.
BEN: What?? Wait…I'm calling.

A second later my phone vibrates in my hand. As soon as I connect the call I can hear Ben laughing. I don't even get a chance to greet him. Mum would be horrified.

"He said what?" He's still laughing.

"It's not funny. It's not even like a normal open relationship. He just said he has a long-standing arrangement with a lady friend and he doesn't plan to end things with her until the day he gets married. They're basically dating without the label."

"Are you serious? He should be on polyamory sites or something."

"Well, the kicker is he doesn't want his girlfriend to have the same arrangement. Apparently the openness only goes in one direction."

"That's a bit hypocritical. Does he really think it's going to be easy to find a girl who's okay with that?"

"That's what I asked! What self-respecting woman would put up with that? I suppose it's not my place to judge. But that's not all—she's married! He's even taking her to Germany for a week."

I know I still sound shocked, but I really can't help it. It genuinely boggles my mind that there are people out there who are fine with these sorts of arrangements.

"No way! I wish I'd been there to see it."

"Did you have the night off work?"

"Yeah, there were a few other things that needed my attention."

With his vague answer I'm suddenly bombarded by the very unwelcome thought of him going on dates with other women. Now *I'm* the one who's being a complete hypocrite. I realize this. Not only do I not have any claim on the guy, but I myself have got plenty of blind dates lined up for the next couple of weeks. I'm as bad as Hugh and his lopsided arrangement. I have no right to be upset at the thought of Ben going on dates himself. He's just my friend after all. I just wish I could get my heart to agree with my head.

"Sounds like you could use my help finding a decent date."

Yep. This attraction is definitely one-sided if he's offering to arrange dates for me. At least he's a fun wingman to have around.

"Ugh. I've already got some lined up for next week. Let's hope they're better than the last three."

"I'll see you Saturday?" His statement is posed as more of a hopeful question and that lifts my spirits.

"Yeah. I'm looking forward to it."

"Me too."

I really need to get these emotions under control where Ben is concerned.

Just a friend. Just a friend. Just a friend.

Maybe if I chant that to myself enough, I'll actually believe it.

CHAPTER EIGHT

BEN ARRIVES to pick me up from Clem and Dan's place bright and early on Saturday.

We both did the sensible thing when you're planning to go sightseeing and wore comfortable sneakers. Ben's wearing a blue Red Sox t-shirt that fits snugly around his biceps and I can't help but enjoy the gun show as he reaches up to remove his sunglasses. He's not body-builder buff like Hugh, but he definitely works out.

He goes in for a hug and I don't stop him. When his arms wrap around me I'm reminded of how good he smells. So so good.

NO! Not good, Callahan! Bad. Very Bad!

Trying to get my wayward thoughts under control is like trying to wrangle a bar of soap in a bathtub. Impossible.

I make some quick introductions, because of course Dan and Clem are loitering around the front door, not keen to pass up the opportunity to meet the man himself. I can see by the little twinkle in her eye that Clem is impressed by what she sees. When Ben is not looking, she gives me a little knowing smirk. Thankfully they make themselves scarce after a brief hello.

"Ready for some sightseeing? I'll park the car. I've got us tickets for the Hop-on Hop-off Trolley. That way we don't have to walk too far."

"Is that because I'm ridiculously unfit?" I ask with a smile.

It was actually really thoughtful of him.

Ben laughs and then looks me up and down, lingering on my legs that are exposed thanks to the sundress I'm wearing. My heart does some kind of strange flutter.

"You look pretty fit to me, Callahan. Do you run?"

This is the first time he's called me Callahan, and my heart does another flip-flop.

"Ha! No. Definitely not! I don't mind walking, or hiking, but you'll never catch me running. Scratch that. I'd run if there were zombies chasing me. Or to save a small child."

Ben grins.

"Only a small one? Not a medium-size child?" he teases. "I actually got the trolley tickets because it's a good way to see a lot in a short amount of time. I don't want you completely exhausted before we even hit Fenway Park. Can't have you falling asleep in the stands at your first Red Sox game. That would be a crime."

***

Our sightseeing begins at the aquarium, which Ben very generously pays for. No matter how much I insist, he won't take any money for the aquarium admission, or for the trolley tickets. I know The Old Copper Pig is really popular, but I don't imagine he makes *that* much money, so I only agree on condition that he lets me pay for lunch and any other entry fees.

By the time we have to head to the Red Sox game, we've seen Faneuil Hall, Paul Revere House, Old North Church, and Old Ironsides, and have taken a brisk walk through the Boston Common and Public Garden.

Even with the trolley tickets, there was a fair amount of walking, so I was very grateful for a pit stop at the Cheers bar, where we had a delicious pub lunch. Thank goodness Ben was organized enough to book a table in advance because the place was packed.

Even with all the tourists milling about, there is something really special about *Beantown*. There is something in the atmosphere that's hard to describe. It reminds me of sitting at an airport people-watching. You can *feel* the excitement in the air.

It's the same here. The rich history and architecture, the cobbled alleys, and beautiful gardens…it's all perfect. I love England, but I could easily spend the rest of my life here.

Fenway Park is packed to the rafters and the air is already thick with the smell of hot dogs, popcorn, and the unmistakable scent of freshly cut grass from the field.

The seats we're in are fairly close to the field in something that Ben refers to as a loge box. I have no idea what that means, all I know is that I have a great view. High enough that I can see what's happening, but not too high that the players look like ants.

"How did you manage to get such great seats?" I ask as we sit down.

"My family has season tickets. We take turns coming to games," Ben says as he opens his backpack and pulls out a Red Sox jersey. "Here. You can't come to a game without showing the proper support."

"Wow! You came prepared. Thanks. Does this belong to you, or one of your brothers?" I ask as I pull the jersey over my sundress.

"No!" Ben laughs. "I'd never be able to convince Connor or Liam to part with their jerseys. They're sacred. I bought it for you."

"Ben!" I feel bad. Even though I did pay for some things, he must have spent an absolute fortune on me today. "You didn't have to do that! Can I at least pay you back?"

"Nope. My treat. Your company is payment enough," he says with a wink.

That just does funny things to my heart, which seems to be flip-flopping in my chest again. I've never been one to find winking attractive, but when Ben does it, there's something super sexy and charming about it.

Friends. Just friends.

I can't lose control every time he says something remotely flirty. I have to keep reminding myself that he isn't looking for anything serious, and he's a barman.

I try to focus on the noise around me while we wait for the game to start. The constant chatter and laughter of the crowd is a good distraction. Children squeal with delight as they race up and down the aisles, while vendors bellow out their wares at the top of their lungs.

As the players take to the field, the energy in the stadium intensifies with cheers. There is something magical about the crack of the bat echoing through the stadium as the ball is sent flying into the air and the crowd erupts in cheers.

Perhaps it's because I'm used to watching rugby matches, but the game feels fairly slow to me, in spite of the electric atmosphere—kind of like cricket, with each side taking turns.

Ben very patiently explains all the rules and terminology. "Innings" is about the only term I understand, thanks to Dad and his love for cricket, although I soon find out there are a lot more innings in baseball than in cricket.

By the end of the game, I still don't really know the infield from the outfield, or what constitutes a foul ball, but I do know what a Fenway Frank tastes like, and I've had an absolute blast.

Ben is the most considerate, sweet date I've ever…no wait, *not a date. He's NOT my date.*

Heaven help me, I'm turning into giggling Courtney. If this was the kind of day he spent with her, no wonder she fell so hard for him.

Let's hope that, unlike Courtney, I can at least control myself over dinner and not paw at him.

***

"So, what are you looking for in these blind dates?" Ben's question comes out of the blue over dinner after the game. We're seated in a quiet booth at the back of a quaint little Italian restaurant in Back Bay.

"Well, if you want to know the truth, I have a list."

I don't know why I'm telling him this. I would blame it on the wine, but I'm drinking water, so really, I have no excuse except that I seem to lose the ability to reason properly when he's around. It's like I lose all filters and spew out whatever I'm thinking.

"A list? Okay, let's hear it." He sounds genuinely interested.

"Firstly, he has to want something serious. Not that I'm saying I'll marry the next guy," I clarify, "but I do want somebody who is serious about dating and is at the settling down stage of their life."

Unlike you. I don't say that bit out loud, but my eyes flick to his for a second and I know he's also thinking about that very first conversation we had although he doesn't make any comment.

"He has to have a stable job."

"That sounds reasonable."

"I believe so. I mean, it's not like I plan to stop working and laze around the house all day for the rest of my life. I just want to know that my husband is earning a decent income. My last boyfriend was a complete freeloader and I've seen how stressful it can be with my aunt. She's spent her life working herself to the bone trying to support her kids and a husband who can't hold down a job for longer than a week. She's supposed to be enjoying retirement by now, but my uncle gambled away all their savings. At least, the savings he hadn't already spent on a couple of mistresses. She'll work until she dies. I don't want that."

More spewing. I just can't help myself. It all just comes pouring out when Ben's around.

"Is this your cousin Clementine's mother?"

I'm impressed that he even remembers Clem's name. After all, the introductions earlier were really brief.

"Good gracious no! Clem's mum, Dorothy, and my mum are sisters and two peas in a pod. Both my dad and Uncle Rupert deserve medals. No, this aunt is my dad's sister. I love her, but she's made some really poor life choices, including her choice in life partner, and she's had to live with the consequences."

"I'm surprised she never left him."

"Not for a lack of trying on my dad's part. He offered to help her out the first time she found out my uncle was cheating, and many times since then, but she's stubborn. And for reasons I'll never quite understand, she loves my uncle in spite of how terribly he's treated her. She'll never leave him." I shake my head and give Ben a sheepish smile. "I must sound like a terrible niece speaking about my uncle this way."

He shakes his head. "Not at all. I would probably feel exactly the same if my uncle cheated on my aunt and gambled away her retirement savings. I understand why you want your future partner to have a good, stable job."

"So you don't think I'm crazy?"

Sometimes I wonder myself. Even Clem thinks this fear that I'm going to end up supporting a mooch of a husband is irrational. I don't wait for him to answer.

"It's not that I need to be wealthy." I feel like I need to clarify this. I don't want him to think I'm some gold-digger. "I just don't want to have to stress about finances."

"There's nothing wrong with wanting financial security and a partner who has a secure job. Especially in this economy, where most people live paycheck to paycheck. So, what else is on this list?"

"A good sense of humor."

"Absolutely essential," Ben agrees with a smile.

"Intelligent. I don't need a rocket scientist, but we need to be able to hold a somewhat intellectually stimulating conversation."

Ben nods. "What else?"

"A family man. It would be nice if he was close to his family. I may tease my mum, but I adore both my parents. Family is really important to me. And obviously I want somebody who also wants kids someday. I want somebody that shares those family values."

"That doesn't sound like an unreasonable list."

"I don't think so either, but for some reason I can't find what I'm looking for. Finding a good man is like trying to find a parking spot at a crowded mall during the Christmas holidays—you know they're out there somewhere, but you can never seem to get your hands on one."

I huff in frustration and Ben chuckles at my dramatics.

"What about you? Why are you so averse to commitment?" I ask.

Ben shakes his head.

"I'm *not* averse to commitment; just the opposite. I take it so seriously because it's a big deal. My brother rushed into a marriage he shouldn't have and ended up divorced at twenty-five. I'm not letting the same thing happen to me."

"So, no serious relationships then?" I'm intrigued. He really seems like good boyfriend material.

"Oh, I've dated women casually, but it never ends well…usually because the women want more than I'm ready to give. I'd happily be in a committed relationship, it's just that I haven't found someone worth committing to yet. I take commitment and marriage seriously, you know? I don't want to blindly stumble into something without genuine love and compatibility. I'm not just going to date anybody. Call me old-fashioned, but I believe in finding that deep connection, that spark that goes beyond just fleeting attraction. I want a partner who understands the value of trust, loyalty, and shared dreams. I want to marry my best friend. Until then, I'll keep searching for someone who truly captures my heart."

I feel a bit chastised, even if that isn't his intent. Am I trying to rush commitment and marriage? Am I really going to find what I'm looking for on a dating app?

"Yeah." I sigh. "Finding somebody like that isn't so easy."

"Hmmm. Maybe it's your initial selection criteria that's the problem. Sounds like you need a wingman. Come on, let's see what you've got on that app." He motions to my phone.

I pick it up and open the dating app as Ben comes around to my side of the booth and plonks his butt down next to me.

I'm scrolling through the list of men I've been talking to but all I can think about is the way Ben's arm is stretched out along the bench behind me.

"These are some of the options," I tell him and slowly swipe through their profiles.

Every now and then he leans in to inspect the phone more closely and his skin makes contact with my back, sending unwelcome tingles through me. I blame all this talk of relationships.

"What about this one? The vet." Ben asks quietly.

I'm trying to focus on the conversation but my mind keeps drifting to the casual brush of his hand near my shoulder and the way his warm breath tickles my neck every time he leans in and speaks.

"I uh…I…have a date set up with him soon actually."

Ben is sitting so close I can hear him breathe. Steady, calm breaths, unlike my erratic breathing. He seems completely unaffected, and here I am, trying desperately to keep my wits about me.

"What about this one?" Ben points at another profile which I had considered, but ultimately decided against. I can still feel the tantalizing sensation of his warm breath as it tickles my cheek and neck like a gentle caress. I suppress a shiver and try to focus.

"I don't know. I mean he seems nice, and we have exactly the same interests, but he works at a department store. That sounds like minimum wage shift work. Doesn't really seem very stable. I don't know…does that make me sound like a snob? I should probably just be grateful he has a job."

"That may not be all he does, and you'll only find out if you get to know him. Kate, life is too short to always play it safe. Sometimes you have to take risks. There's nothing wrong with wanting some financial security, but don't be so rigid that you let that stop you from missing out on something good."

His gentle but serious tone makes me turn my head slightly to look at him.

I realize my mistake too late. *A BIG mistake.*

His face is right there in front of me and I may just melt under the intensity of his gaze.

His lips are dangerously close to mine and I can practically feel the electricity zinging through the air. I wonder what his response would be if I leaned forward and laid one on him. I'm fighting the urge to grab his shirt and pull him close. I don't know how much self-control I've got left in me.

I'm saved from embarrassing myself when Ben abruptly pulls back before going and sitting back on the other side of the booth, breaking the tension.

I let out a long, shaky breath. I'm actually starting to feel sorry for poor Courtney. No wonder she couldn't keep her hands to herself.

CHAPTER NINE

"YOU TOLD him about the list?"

It's Sunday brunch with Clem, Dan, and the kids, and while we're sitting in the sunshine eating, I'm filling my cousin in on the latest disastrous date and my not-date with Ben.

"What list?"

Dan is not above eavesdropping.

I spend the next ten minutes filling Dan in on *the list*.

Dan is not a man of many words, so when he starts giving me a lecture I just about fall off my chair in shock.

"You know what you need to do Kate?" he asks, pointing his fork in my direction before spearing a hash brown with some force. "Tear it up. You don't need a list. I know you. You'll end up so obsessed with the thing that you'll end up missing out on something good. You should be following your heart, not dating somebody because they fill some boxes on your checklist."

"I don't think it's an unreasonable list."

If I sound defensive and a little bit put out, it's because I am. I suppose he has a point. I do tend to get a little neurotic about things. I'm the first one to acknowledge I'm a bit of a control freak. But I don't think that's what I'm doing here.

"You can't tell me there weren't specific things you were looking for in a wife before you met Clementine?"

He swallows and pins me to my chair with an unimpressed look.

"I wasn't even thinking about marriage before Clementine. I followed my heart when I met your cousin, and she's the best thing that ever happened to me."

I'd be tempted to punch him if that wasn't so romantic and sweet. My cousin obviously thinks so too because she gives him a kiss on the cheek.

"Aw, babe, you're so romantic."

Clem's swooning is interrupted by Temper Trap's *Sweet Disposition*. It's the ringtone for my mum and the irony of my choice always makes me smile.

"Hello my pet." Surprisingly, it's Dad's voice I hear on the other end.

"Hello Dad. Is Mum still not over our little tiff?" My mum didn't speak to me during last week's Sunday call. She's still in a huff about the internet dating thing.

"She's still *pretending* she's not over it," Dad says and I can hear Mum grumbling in the background. "She's also pretending that she's not interested in how the latest date went and your day out with Ben. She's practically bursting at the seams with curiosity."

More grumbling in the background.

"How does she know about my day out with Ben?"

"Clem told Aunty Dot, and of course she told your mum."

I narrow my eyes at Clementine. She obviously knew exactly how my dad would answer that question because she gives me a cheeky grin and sticks out her tongue, which makes me roll my eyes.

This family is ridiculous. You can't have any secrets.

"Well, you can tell Mum that the date was a disaster. Again. He was nice enough, until he told me he has a Wednesday night friends-with-benefits arrangement that he doesn't plan to give up."

"What's a friends-with-ben—" Dad doesn't even get a chance to finish his question before Mum is panting down the line like she's just run a marathon.

"He has a friends-with-benefits arrangement with somebody?" She's shocked.

I was obviously talking loudly enough that she could hear my end of the conversation clearly. I can just imagine the way she snatched the phone out of poor Dad's hand.

I ignore her question and ask one of my own. "So, are you over our little spat Mum?"

"Never mind about that darling…he has a friend-with-benefits?

Well, I never! I thought that kind of thing only happened in films. Did you know that, Harold?" I'm forgotten for a second as Mum talks to Dad. "Friends-with-benefits. That's when they have sexual relations with a friend. You know, a no-strings-attached arrangement? You know like that film we watched…what was it called?"

I can just picture Mum doing air quotes as she explains to Dad what a friend-with-benefits is.

"Yes Mum, and you'll be thrilled to know that I told him I wasn't interested."

"Well, I should hope so Catherine! I raised you better than that darling. I still think you need to meet a nice young man at church."

"It gets worse, Mum." Felicity Callahan loves a bit of drama. She may not like me meeting strangers from the internet, but she's as desperate to hear about my dating misadventures as Alex is. They'd get along famously.

"No! Why? What happened?" She's enraptured by the conversation. I bet she's leaning forward in her special chair.

"His *friend* is actually married." There's a shriek on the other end. "Never!"

"True. And not only is he taking her on holiday to Germany, but her husband knows, and he doesn't care."

"Scandalous! Disgraceful. Wait until Aunty Dot hears about this! It sounds like something you would see on the telly. Like an episode of *Made in Chelsea*!"

With Mum's penchant for gossip and a bit of drama, she loves shows like that, which I find quite amusing because it seems so at odds with the posh side of her.

"One would hope that men would be a little more discriminating when it comes to where they put their…uh…twig and berries."

"Mother!" Now it's my turn to shriek at my very prim and proper mother. "Please don't *ever* say that again. I don't ever want to be discussing *anybody's* twig and berries with you."

Ugh. I wish I could unhear that. I need some mind bleach!

While I'm thinking about how this conversation is going to scar me for life, Clementine is cackling beside me, clearly keeping track of the conversation. I give her another unimpressed look, which only makes her laugh harder.

"I'm just saying, sweetheart, I do hope that not all these interweb men you meet are as sordid as this chap."

"They're not, Mum. I've got two dates lined up for this week and they both sound like a frightful bore. You'd love them," I add with a grin, because although Mum loves a bit of scandal, she doesn't want that for her daughter. No, in *real life*, she likes rules and order…except when she and Aunty Dot have had one too many Pimm's Cups to drink, then all bets are off.

Mum lets out a little huff of annoyance. "Don't be cheeky. I won't babysit your children one day."

Now that makes me laugh.

"Mum, ocean away or not, I couldn't keep you away from your grandchildren if I tried. Don't go making idle threats. Does Dad want to talk?"

"No." Now she's the one laughing. "He disappeared the moment I said 'sexual relations'. I don't think he wanted to be a part of that conversation."

I feel his pain. At least he missed the twig and berries part.

"And how was your day out with Ben?"

"Now that was a different story altogether. It was awesome."

I spend the rest of the call giving my mum the cliff notes, trying desperately not to sound like a giddy teenager every time I talk about how thoughtful and sweet he was.

***

"Is that 'im? Date number four?" Alex leans over my shoulder to get a better look at the profile picture of date number four, Mike. I'm meeting him tomorrow after work, just for drinks.

Unlike most of the guys I've met on this dating site, Mike seems almost a bit reluctant. I'm not sure why. He's the one who contacted me first. Maybe he's just a bit shy.

"Yes." I shove a huge forkful of lettuce in my mouth while Alex continues his close-up inspection of my laptop.

If I'm going to keep eating out on all these dates I'm going to have to survive on lunches of salads and soups for the foreseeable future. It's either that or more hours in the gym, and I'm already there too often for my liking.

"Oooh, he looks lovely." Viola joins in on the inspection.

"Let's 'ope 'e is better than number three, yes?" Alex's high-pitched laugh peels through the open-plan office.

As I anticipated, Alex was hanging on my every word when I told him about Hugh and his lady friend. He even clapped his hands together like a happy seal. I knew the details would delight him. After that debacle I'm actually quite looking forward to my Wednesday night date.

"Well, speak of the devil…" I speak through a mouthful of salad as I look at my phone which is vibrating all over my desk.

It's a good thing my mum isn't here to observe my bad manners. I hope he isn't phoning to cancel.

"Hi, Mike." Thankfully I managed to swallow before I answered.

For a change, Alex is giving me some privacy and is actually doing some work.

"Hi, Kate. I, uh, wanted to speak with you about something important before our date tomorrow."

He sounds nervous. My stomach drops because this conversation doesn't sound like it's heading in a good direction.

"Okay." Only, I'm not sure that it is okay. Not sure at all. "What is it?"

"Well, I, um, I'm not really sure how to tell you this. But, uh, I wanted to give you a chance to back out now if you still wanted…I mean, after you find out."

He's fumbling over his words and even though I desperately want to tell him to go on and spit it out, I just wait patiently for him to continue.

"The thing is…well, the thing is that I have a paraphilic infantilism fetish." The words come rushing out fast.

"Uhm…"

He can obviously hear I have no idea what that is.

"Basically, when I'm in the privacy of my own home I, uh… I like to wear a diaper and pretend to be a baby. Not just occasionally. I mean, regularly. It's something that's a big part of my life."

It's a good thing I had already swallowed, because if I hadn't, I would have had a mouthful of salad all over my laptop by now. As it is, I'm trying not to choke on my own saliva.

"Uh…mmm, I, um." I can't seem to form a coherent sentence.

Of all the things he could possibly have told me, I never in a million years would have guessed that this would be it.

"Look, I totally understand if you'd rather cancel. I mean, I'd be disappointed of course, but I know that's not something everybody is comfortable with and that's okay. I just felt it was only fair to tell you beforehand."

There is an awkward silence before I finally manage to splutter a reply.

"Mike, I…thank you for telling me." The heavy sigh that escapes my lips cannot be helped. I really respect him for being upfront and honest, but I can't help but feel totally deflated. "I feel bad about it, but you're right, this isn't something I'd be comfortable with in a relationship. I'm really sorry, but I do really appreciate you telling me."

It's true. I'm massively relieved that he told me upfront, but that's *really* not something I ever want to have to deal with. It definitely doesn't fit the list. I'm looking for just your boring, baggage-free, average Joe.

When the call ends, I drop my head to my desk. A few times.

"So, what did 'e say?" Alex's head peers over the partition again, observing me thumping my head with a frown. I don't have the energy to give him the details and besides, I would feel like I was violating Mike's privacy.

Before I have a chance to reply, my phone pings with a message.

Hugh: I had an amazing time on our date. You're amazing. I haven't felt chemistry like this before. I'm not giving up. Hope you'll at least think about what we talked about.

Oh no. I need to make it clear to Hugh that in spite of the chemistry, there is no chance I'll change my mind.

I let out a long sigh as I tweak my termination message, as Clem likes to call it, and send it to Hugh.

When I look up, I see Alex is still waiting for a response.

"I just want normal, boring, stable. Is that too much to ask?" The pout I'm giving him obviously makes me look like a sad, lost puppy, because he pats my head as if I am one.

Viola gets up on the way to the copier and gives my shoulder a squeeze. "Chin up, buttercup. It can only get better from here, right?"

"At least you still 'ave date number five to look forward to, *ma cherie*. Maybe 'e will be *the one*. *Oui?*"

CHAPTER TEN

HE'S definitely NOT *the one*.

Randy is short, stocky, and balding on the top but has tried to cover it with a terrible comb-over. He's also wearing glasses that look way too big for his face and has a belly that hangs over his belt.

Not only is he a lot older than his profile picture, but there is only a very vague resemblance. *Very vague*. The way a hairless cat resembles a lion.

I genuinely thought the wrong person had sat down in front of me and was about to say, "Sorry, I'm waiting for somebody," when he introduced himself.

If I hadn't already been sitting down I might have fallen over.

For the last five minutes, I haven't heard a word he's said because all I can think about is how different he looks from his picture.

I feel like it may be a bit rude and confrontational to point out, and normally I avoid confrontation at all costs, but after a few minutes of ruminating over it, I just can't let it go.

"Randy, I have to admit, you look nothing like your profile picture."

He laughs, which comes out as a bit of a snort.

"I know. It's my cousin. I find nobody really shows any interest if I use my own photos."

He sounds completely unashamed of his deceit.

"But…it's wrong. It's not you, and they're going to find out anyway when you go on a date."

"But by that time, they'll have gotten to know me more, and what's not to love?"

He wiggles his eyebrows in what he probably thinks is a charming manner, and I force a smile, feeling more uncomfortable by the minute.

He launches back into a monologue and my mind wanders again.

I've only just met him and I realize that judging him solely based on his looks is shallow—I admit it, I'm shallow. But surely there has to be at least *some* physical attraction for a relationship to work?

I take a sip of my water and look around the restaurant. There is gaudy red velvet on the chairs and lighting to match.

I'm sure the date would be a little more bearable if we were at The Old Copper Pig. Instead, we're at a crowded restaurant a block away and I'm listening to Randy very animatedly explain his theory on why women are afraid of commitment, why they're overly emotional, and why they've never done anything of great significance in the world.

I'm trying to look past the misogynistic comments, but it's difficult. He's throwing up red flags all over the place and it's taking all my willpower not to just get up and walk out.

I can't even get a question in because he's spent almost the entire date talking about himself (occasionally even in the third person). It's hard not to keep tuning out.

"…and that's how Randy saved the raccoon's life. You know, some people call me a hero. I'd never call myself one of course, but you know, that's what everybody else says. A real-life hero."

One of the reasons I liked his profile was because he's a veterinarian. A nice, stable job. And a guy who loves animals? Winner! Even Ben pointed out his profile. It looked very promising.

Well, that's what I thought until I met Randy. Now I'm going to have to rethink that. I don't think he loves the animals nearly as much as he loves himself. At least he's off his "the problem with women…" topic.

Fudge nuggets. I'm on a date with a pompous, self-centered misogynist. It can't end soon enough.

***

After another disappointing date I feel like talking to Ben, which is why I find myself pushing open the door of my preferred stamping ground and scanning the bar for my favorite bartender.

He's not behind the bar, so perhaps he isn't working tonight. I'm about to turn around and leave when I hear him call my name as he makes his way between tables.

"Hey. How's my favorite expat?"

He gives me a hug, tucking my head under his chin, and I hold on a little bit longer than strictly necessary because his leather and soap smell is just so comforting. Hopefully he didn't notice.

Our day out seems have really solidified the friendship. He's become more affectionate and I'm here for it!

"How was the date? It was the vet, right?"

"Yes, it was the vet. The best part was the part when I left. But I survived," I reply, as I pull away from his chest.

Ben high-fives me and I can't help but laugh at the gesture.

"What was that for?"

"Because you're a survivor."

He's corny and cute.

"So, what happened? What was wrong with this guy?"

"Have you ever watched *Seinfeld*? This guy was George Costanza in the flesh. Down to the balding head and glasses, the only difference is this guy had a terrible comb-over to try hide his balding. He even spoke like George."

I wonder if I would've been able to get past the looks if he'd had a winning personality. Sadly, his personality was insufferable. He was self-absorbed, dishonest, and negative about everything (except himself, of course).

"I can't decide if Randy is a terrible name for him, or if it's perfectly suited. On one hand, he's not randy at all if his 'the problem with women…' speeches are anything to go by. But he kept wiggling his eyebrows in this suggestive way, so maybe it's a perfect fit."

"It could be worse. He could've had a strange fetish," Ben says.

I'm instantly reminded of my conversation with Mike.

"He may well have, but I was too afraid to ask. Maybe he likes to roleplay being a hero. He talked enough about how everybody thinks he's a hero. He wouldn't call himself that, of course. No, no. It's everybody else who calls him a hero. He probably makes his partner pretend to be an injured raccoon or something."

Ben tries, unsuccessfully, to hold in his laughter.

"I'm sorry," he says wiping his eye. "I shouldn't be laughing. That sounds like a traumatic date."

His laughter is so infectious I can't help but laugh along with him.

I'm about to head for the bar so that I can talk to him while he works, when he says, "Come on, let's go for a walk."

Ben takes me by the elbow and steers me out of the restaurant before linking my arm through his.

"Don't you need to work?"

"Nope. What about your Wednesday night date?"

A great big sigh rushes out of my mouth.

"It never happened. On the subject of fetishes…he phoned me the day before to tell me he likes to wear diapers and pretend to be a baby in the privacy of his own home. He was giving me a chance to back out."

I expect him to laugh at this turn of events too, especially considering we were just joking about fetishes, but he doesn't. He just looks surprised.

"Really? Well, that was decent of him, I guess," Ben says after taking a moment to absorb what I just told him.

"Yeah. I did appreciate that. The thing is, I just want normal. Why is it so hard to find normal?"

Ben looks down at me with a slight frown. "Define normal."

"Well, I want an average Joe. Somebody that fits the list obviously, but I don't want weird habits, strange kinks, or complicated relationship history. I just want normal."

He moves his arm around my shoulder and gives me a squeeze. "Don't worry, you'll find what you're looking for."

"I hope so. I might have to just kiss a few frogs until then."

"No! No kissing anything." Ben laughs and swiftly changes the topic. "So when am I going to introduce you to the magic that is Mario Kart?"

On our sightseeing day, he was horrified to find out that I not only had never heard of Mario Kart, but I've also never touched a Nintendo or PlayStation console.

It is a little surprising, considering Johnny was attached to his PlayStation at the hip. Although, he never attempted to include me in that part of his life.

"You tell me, Jeff Gordon."

If his self-proclaimed mad Mario Kart skills are anything to go by, Ben is a driving legend.

"How about next week Wednesday at my place? We can make it

a game and movie night."
"That sounds good. But I get to pick the movie."
"And when are we going apartment hunting for you?"

63

CHAPTER ELEVEN

IT TURNS out that apartment hunting in Boston is a breeze when Ben's around. I'd told him that I'd been dreading trying to find an apartment. I didn't particularly want to share a place, if I could help it, but just looking at some of the places available online made me realize I may need to sell an organ to be able to afford a one-bedroom apartment in a decent part of the city.

Things within my budget seemed to be either in a not-so-desirable part of the city, or the size of a closet. Boston is not a cheap city, so when Ben said his friend is a real estate agent who could show me a place within my budget, I'd been less than enthusiastic. The only reason I agreed is because it isn't fair on Clem and Dan to spend another couple of months in their guest room.

When we pull up to the apartment building I'm pleasantly surprised.

The apartment is in an old brownstone on a tree-lined street in a swanky part of the city. It doesn't hurt that it's also not far from The Old Copper Pig.

There's no way I'll be able to afford this. We're talking Back Bay, Beacon Hill kind of luxury.

"Are you sure this is in my budget?"

Ben clocks the dubious look on my face as we get out of the car.

"Stop stressing. I promise it's within your budget," he reassures me as we walk up the stairs to greet his realtor friend, Jackson.

After introductions are made, he takes us up to the second-floor apartment and I'm blown away.

The inside of the apartment looks like something out of a magazine. The old exterior belies the modern interior which has been tastefully furnished. Although the décor is primarily neutrals, it's not cold or clinical. There's something very warm and inviting about it.

There is an open-concept kitchen and living room with large windows, making it feel light and spacious. There's only one bedroom with a full bathroom, but the living room has a little desk nook that can function as a workspace. There is ample closet space and best of all, it comes fully furnished. It's heavenly.

"When you said you had the perfect place for me I didn't realize you meant a luxury condo. This is gorgeous, Jackson. How can I possibly afford this? There is no way this is within my budget."

If I thought I had to sell a kidney to afford some of the other places I've looked at…I may have to part with a few different organs to be able to afford this upscale apartment.

Jackson glances at Ben before answering my question.

"Well, there is one small catch…"

"I *knew* there had to be something wrong. Go on then." I sigh.

Jackson laughs.

"It's really not bad. You see, the apartments in the building are still under development. They're being completely renovated. This is the first apartment that's been completed as a show home to show prospective buyers what their money can buy them. They get to choose the finishes in their own apartment. The catch is that you'll have to put up with some construction noise, and occasionally let me show potential buyers the apartment, which means keeping it clean. Don't worry, though. I promise to give you plenty of warning, and best of all, you can move in immediately. I can give you the keys right now, if you'd like."

I think my grin is so wide my face might split.

"As far as catches go, that's a pretty sweet deal. Where do I sign?"

***

When I pull up in front of Ben's building on Wednesday evening for our game night, I wonder if he got a similar sweet deal on his lease because his apartment is even better than mine.

It's also a gorgeous old brownstone which, judging by the

number of buzzers at the front door, has been divided into four apartments. That means one per floor, so it must be a lot bigger than mine. It's only a couple of blocks from my own, in a very sought-after street.

Ben buzzes me in and I take the stairs to the top floor, my leg muscles protesting all the way.

I never should have agreed to play racquetball with Clementine yesterday evening. She needed a night off from the kids but instead of just having drinks or dinner like normal people, she insisted we do something that involved cardio.

I've never played racquetball in my life but Clem insisted that it was just like the squash we played as teenagers. And just like when we were teens, Clementine absolutely thrashed me. By the end of the evening my legs were barely functioning. She had to pull me by the arms and drag me off the court like a naughty toddler.

By the time I get to the top floor, I'm huffing and puffing. No wonder Ben is so fit walking up and down these stairs every day.

When I reach the landing at the top the door is open and Ben is standing with his arms folded and a big grin on his face. He must have heard the groaning.

"Racquetball?"

I had informed him of my complete annihilation on the court via text.

"Why couldn't you live on the bottom floor? I don't think I'm going to make it," I say with a groan as I sway a little.

Ben laughs and before I know what's happening he's swept me right off my feet and is carrying me to the living room, bridal style.

Normally I'd be swooning at the move. *Swooning!* But I'm in too much pain to properly appreciate the show of masculine strength that normally sends ovaries into overdrive.

"I thought you said your mother was the dramatic one."

"Hey!" I give his upper arm a little pinch. Well, I try to, but it's not easy because there's nothing there but solid muscle. "I thought I was going to fall."

"You'll never fall when you're with me, Callahan."

Could he be any cuter?

I take advantage of the fact that I'm in his arms and lean in very slightly, giving his neck a stealthy little sniff.

So yummy!

I need to find out what body wash he uses.

"Did you just sniff me?"

"Uh…no?" Apparently not stealthy enough.

Ben only chuckles as he deposits me on the couch.

Looking around, I can see I was right. He's a bartender with a sweet apartment like this? Jackson definitely hooked him up with a rental deal like mine. Either that, or he's moonlighting as a drug dealer. This place is fantastic.

There are already cartons of Chinese food sitting on the coffee table and they smell divine. After that grueling climb up the stairs my body is crying out for sustenance.

"Help yourself."

Ben obviously notices my eyes are glued to the Chinese food. Or perhaps he heard my stomach rumbling.

As I tuck into my beef and broccoli, I ask Ben about his day and he tells me about having to dodge Courtney at the grocery store. He was saved from an unfortunate run in by ducking behind a cereal display to avoid her.

Poor Courtney. After spending the day with Ben I've had a complete turn-around in my attitude towards her. I still think she was very rude, and I don't like the idea of her pawing Ben, but you can't really blame the girl.

When we're done eating, Ben clears everything away and hands me a game controller of some kind.

"You ready to be crushed, Callahan?"

"Bring it on."

It turns out Mario Kart is a super fun game and in spite of my shrieks and squeals, it's actually a great stress-reliever. I should do this more often.

I'm not completely terrible at it. I even manage to win a couple of rounds, but for the most part, I am well and truly crushed.

"So what are we watching?" Ben asks as we settle on the couch.

"*Father of the Bride*. A classic."

I've watched it dozens of times. So many that I can recite most of the lines. I love all the characters, especially the wacky wedding planner Franck now that I live in Boston, because he's a German version of Alex.

"I should have guessed it would be a mushy romcom."

I give him a nudge with my elbow.

"You got a problem with that, Ben? Not manly enough for you?"

He bumps me right back before stretching his arms out across the back of the couch.

"Not at all, Callahan. Not at all. I actually *love* romcoms."

He says it with such a straight face that I can't tell if he's joking or not.

CHAPTER TWELVE

I DUMP my laptop bag on my desk before slumping in my chair, noting on my little desk clock that I'm just on time today.

"'ello, Catherine." I smile at the sound of Alex's voice coming from the other side of the partition.

He loves to use my full name, although pronounced the French way, it sounds more like cat-a-reen. On the rare occasion that he does use Kate, it sounds more like cat, which I find amusing. Even when he is up in my business.

"Hey, Kate! So, how was your movie and game night with Ben last night?"

For a change, it's Viola whose asking and not the little French gossipmonger. Although his head does pop up in his usual meerkat manner as soon as he hears the question, which leads me to believe that he had forgotten all about it.

"It was great. We ate Chinese, played Mario Kart, and watched *Father of the Bride.*"

"That sounds fun."

"And? What else 'appened?"

"Nothing else happened. What else did you expect? I told you, he's *just* a friend."

I give him the side-eye.

"Hmmm." Alex doesn't seem convinced as his head slowly lowers back down.

"…although, I did end up falling asleep on his couch during the movie."

And, up it pops again!

"*Oooh là là! Romantique.*"

"I wouldn't really call it romantic, especially because when I woke up at 5 a.m. I had drool hanging out of my mouth."

Alex makes a face and Viola chuckles.

"Although, he'd put a pillow under my head and covered me with a blanket which was thoughtful."

"Aw, that's sweet. I'm surprised he didn't wake you when the movie was over," Viola says.

"He said I looked too peaceful to wake up and it was already 1 a.m. He didn't want me driving home so late when I was tired. I rushed home at six to change."

"'e thinks drool 'anging out of your mouth looks peaceful?" Alex makes another face. "It must be *love*. Are you sure you still want to go on your blind date tomorrow?"

I throw a pen in his direction.

"Get back to work, you nosy parker."

Alex just laughs.

***

It's Friday night and once again I'm sitting somewhere other than The Old Copper Pig, opposite Carter the quarterback.

Well, former quarterback. He's now a project manager at a large construction company. The quarterback thing was during his high school and college days and for the last twenty minutes he has been reliving those glory days in vivid detail.

Unfortunately, my lack of any football knowledge whatsoever means I can't contribute meaningfully to the conversation. I just make some vague noises and gestures, indicating agreement and nod my head now and then.

I really should brush up on that knowledge though. Most of my own clients are actors or singers, but a number of Pied Piper's clients are professional football players or other professional sportsmen, like Noah King. I should probably look into American sports in general.

Aside from all the football talk, Carter actually seems like a really nice guy. He's a cute blonde with a very nice jawline, and he's easy to talk to. This date has potential.

We're sitting in a beautiful but crowded little Indian restaurant in the hub of the city. Carter insisted that this place has the best Indian food in Boston.

I'm not sold on the idea. Not because I don't like Indian cuisine. In fact, I love Indian food. It's probably my favorite kind of food. Rather, it has everything to do with the fact that my intestines and my taste buds can't seem to come to any agreement on the issue of spicy food of any kind, be it Indian, Mexican, Chinese. It doesn't matter. While my taste buds rejoice, my intestines quite often lead an unhappy revolt which results in said spicy food making a hasty exit.

The last time I had any Indian food it was a delicious Mughlai chicken curry from the best Indian restaurant in Covent Garden. It did not end well. Let's just say, I became intimately acquainted with every public restroom on the route between the restaurant and my London flat.

But I didn't want to be *that girl*, so I wasn't going to argue about restaurants when he suggested this place. Besides, Ben told me this place was renowned for their fabulous north Indian cuisine.

In an effort to avoid a repeat of the Covent Garden incident, I make a point of ordering the least spicy thing on the menu and I pad my order with plenty of garlic naan.

The names of the dishes on the menu are all unrecognizable, but thankfully they are numbered and the menu has little chilies next to each item, which makes the job of choosing easy with only a brief glance at the menu.

The place is packed, which means we have to wait a while for the food, but I've been told that it's worth it.

The waiter finally sets down our dishes and the tantalizing symphony of flavors smells heavenly.

I listen to Carter talk more about football as I raise the spoon to my mouth and get my first taste of the stew-like dish in front of me.

And then I cough. And cough. And cough some more.

It's rich and flavorful but oh so spicy! The whole inside of my mouth is tingling.

An alarmed-looking Carter comes around to my side of the table and gives me a few firm whacks on the back.

"Are you okay? Are you choking?"

"Fine." I can hardly get the word out as I wave him away.

Sweat beads on my forehead as I reach for my glass of water and gulp it down. It doesn't really help so I stuff a big wad of garlic naan in my mouth and chew. Very unladylike. Mum wouldn't be impressed, but at least it's helping.

"Spicy. So spicy," I finally manage to get out as Carter takes his seat again.

The moment I tasted it, I realized I'd made a terrible mistake. Looking at the menu that's plastered on the wall in large print only confirms my suspicions.

Instead of ordering the dish with just half a chili, I've accidentally ordered the item below it—a whopping five chilies. That's the most there are!

I share this new-found knowledge with Carter.

"I thought you were pretty hard-core ordering their famous Inferno Curry."

"Inferno Curry?" I wail. "Why doesn't it say that on the menu?"

Carter shrugs. "Everybody knows that's their Inferno Curry. They're like, famous for it. They use it in an annual spicy food contest. People come from all over the state for the event."

This is a catastrophe of epic proportions! But honestly, in spite of my initial coughing fit and still-tingling mouth, it's delicious. Ben was right. This place is amazing.

I'm waging an internal war. The initial shock to the system has worn off. My mouth is numb enough not to feel as much of the heat anymore, but I'm still able to appreciate the flavors. But I know what happens when I eat food this spicy. It's not my friend. The battle in my mind is going to end up migrating further south. And quickly too. It's probably not the wisest move to eat the dish.

On the other hand, I don't want to waste food either. Who would waste something so delicious? Plus, it's already been paid for. Growing up, I had enough speeches about starving children in Africa to know that you don't waste food. Not on Felicity Callahan's watch anyway.

I'll only eat half of it. That's a good compromise.

While we eat, I ask him about his work, and he tells me about the various construction projects they're working on at the moment.

When there is a small lull in conversation, I worry that he's going to go back to more football talk, but he surprises me.

"Tell me about your work."

So in between mouthfuls of this spicy goodness, I tell Carter about what I do for a living.

"I know a lot of professional football players who have

publicists."

Aaaand, just like that, we're back to football.

While Carter is talking animatedly about a famous football player I've never heard of, I look down at my almost-empty bowl, realizing that I've eaten way more than I had originally intended to. WAY more. *Oops.*

I silently pray that there are no unpleasant ramifications from my lack of self-control.

"So Carter, tell me, what made you decide to try internet dating?" I ask, trying to steer the conversation away from football again.

It's like the light in his eyes is suddenly extinguished and his shoulders visibly tense. I've clearly said the wrong thing, but I have no idea what. I mean, we did meet online, after all, so you wouldn't think it's a taboo topic. Things have been going well so far. His response is a complete change from the relaxed conversation we've enjoyed up to this point.

He starts to fidget awkwardly with the napkin that's on the table before he finally sighs and answers.

"It seemed like a good option because…I'll never be able to have the woman I really want."

He sounds utterly forlorn and can't even make eye contact. The poor bloke is clearly suffering from a case of unrequited love. Or something of that nature.

Seeing that I don't intend to be anybody's second choice, I immediately decide that this relationship isn't going anywhere. However, I'm also a sucker for a good love story and maybe I can help Carter get a happy ending somehow. I'm not really sure how I can help other than perhaps giving some sage advice, but it's worth a shot.

"Does she know how you feel? Is she in a relationship with somebody else?"

It's only when Carter looks upwards and blinks furiously that I notice his glassy eyes.

"She's married…"

Oh dear. Well, that does put a wrench in the works. I definitely won't be encouraging any kind of homewrecking, so I try to think of a sensible response. I wonder if he works with her.

"Maybe if you put a little bit of distance between—" I don't get to finish that thought before he drops a bombshell with the rest of his declaration.

"…to my brother."

And that statement just opens up the floodgates. Carter the quarterback is sobbing. Body-wracking, heart-wrenching sobs.

"I'm, com-completely in l-l-love with my s-sister-in-law."

I can only just make out the stammering confession which is being muffled by the napkin covering his face.

I've never liked being the center of attention, which may seem strange for somebody whose job is public relations. In spite of my job dealing with people all day, I'm an introvert at heart. Under normal circumstances, the kind of attention his wailing is currently attracting would make me feel very uncomfortable. However, the scene before me is so hopeless and moving that I find myself starting to tear up too.

The poor bloke is in love with his sister-in-law.

"I'm so s-sorry." He furiously rubs at his face, trying to get his breathing under control. "I'm not normally like this. I promise. I just…"

"It's okay, really. Please don't worry about it."

I feel so bad for the poor chap. I mean, football talk aside, he genuinely seems like a lovely guy. He's a nice guy who's fallen in love with a woman he can never have. How tragic.

A quick scan of the room confirms that we are indeed on the receiving end of curious stares. With tears in my eyes and a sniveling date, they're probably thinking we're having an awful row.

"I'm sorry. This is the first date I've been on in a very long time. I thought that if I dated, maybe it would help me get over her. I guess it's not so easy getting over somebody you've loved for the last five years." He sighs. "Would you mind if I cut this date short?" he asks, sniffing and wiping away the trail of moisture that lingers on his face.

"Oh, sure. Of course."

He's probably dying of embarrassment and wants to leg it out of here and hide under the covers for a week. Well, that's what I would be doing.

CHAPTER THIRTEEN

AFTER MY disastrous date with Carter, I sit in my car, thinking about his situation.

I'm so grateful that even though this blind date was another flop, at least I'm not hopelessly in love with my brother-in-law. Poor Carter.

I turn the key in the ignition and nothing happens. Just an ominous sounding click. After trying a few times, I realize this car is not going anywhere anytime soon.

As I lack any mechanical skills whatsoever, I find myself in a bit of a pickle.

What am I supposed to do? Does my car insurance cover roadside assistance? I'm sure it does, but what number do I call to even get assistance?

I should have asked Dan these things weeks ago when I first bought my little car and he arranged the insurance, but when you move to a new country there are a hundred and one important things you don't think to ask until you find yourself in a situation that requires you to *know* said important things.

I can't even phone Dan for help because he's away at a business conference and I can't exactly ask Clem to come rescue me with three-year-old twins in tow. They'll already be fast asleep by now.

I could leave the car here and catch the T, but it's bound to get towed and that will just cause another headache. I should probably have taken the T in the first place.

My mind is suddenly assaulted with unwelcome thoughts of being raped and murdered in an alley. I'm being ridiculous and I know it. Although it's late, the streets are still bustling with activity as people spill out of restaurants and bars, chatting happily.

Okay Kate, you are a grown, independent woman. There's no need to panic.

I mentally scroll through the list of people I could phone for help. It's a short list.

My best bet is definitely my new bestie, Ben. Both The Old Copper Pig and his apartment are not too far from here so hopefully he'll be able to come get me.

I pull out my phone and quickly send Ben an SOS text.

BEN: Sit tight. Leaving TOCP now. I'll be there in 10.

Ben's quick response draws a sigh of relief. He's coming and everything will be okay.

Less than ten minutes later, I see Ben pulling up behind me and get out of my car to greet him.

"Your knight in shining armor has arrived," Ben jokes as he gives me a quick hug before checking out the car.

I'm not exactly sure what he's doing, but after a few minutes of fiddling about under the hood, he declares that it will need to go to a mechanic and makes all the arrangements for me with a few quick phone calls.

Now, I'm not some helpless female that needs a man to rescue her. I've managed quite well on my own for the last decade (Johnny was completely useless and doesn't count). I may not know a carburetor from a radiator, but I'm normally quite capable of getting a mechanic to deal with that stuff for me. I'm independent. I am a woman, hear me roar, and all that jazz. But there's something quite overwhelming about being in a new country where you don't know how things are done, so I'd be lying if I said I didn't feel an immense sense of comfort and relief having Ben around. He may not fit the list, but he's the best friend ever.

"Thanks for rescuing me. I owe you one," I say as we watch the tow truck hook up my car.

"Yes you do. I get to choose the movie on our next movie night," he says with a grin.

Excitement zips through me at his words. Our next movie night? I love that he's talking as if he plans for our movie night to be a regular thing. Thinking about creating a little tradition with Ben shouldn't thrill me so much. After all, friends have traditions too.

Cool your jets, Callahan!

I've been spending so much time with Ben my subconscious is even using Ben's nickname for me.

"That sounds like a fair deal."

I suddenly feel exhausted. I yawn, probably wide enough to swallow a person whole, as the tow truck pulls away with my car. At least I remembered my manners and put my hand over my mouth while I did it.

"Come on, sleepyhead. Let's get you home," Ben says as he puts one arm around my shoulders and steers us towards his car, which is a pretty sweet ride for a bartender.

It wasn't the same car he used to pick me up from Clem's. Either he borrowed it, or he must make a killing in tips. Looking at his gorgeous face, I decide that it's not a far-fetched idea. I'm sure all the ladies love him. Plus, if Jackson hooked him up with a good deal on his apartment like mine, the savings probably means he can afford higher payments on a car.

"Are you finished your shift? I'm really sorry to pull you away from work." I feel bad inconveniencing him like this.

"It's not a problem at all. Really," he says when he spots my dubious look.

"You're going to end up getting fired because of me." Then I'll really feel terrible.

"Nonsense." Ben laughs like the thought is completely absurd. "Who's going to fire me? My hours are completely flexible."

As we pull out smoothly into the road my stomach makes an awfully loud gurgling grumble before I'm hit with the most horrendous stomach cramp.

"Oooh."

I clutch at my stomach and silently pray that I make it home in time because I know exactly what's coming.

What was I thinking eating the Inferno Curry? I must be mad.

Ben's head jerks in my direction. "What is it? Are you okay?"

"Home. Oooh. Need to get home fast."

The words escape through my gritted teeth and are punctuated by moans. I feel like I'm being stabbed by tiny knives. The pain that shoots through me with every cramp is unbearable. I've never been in labor, but I'm pretty sure this must come close. It's like all of my insides are seizing up at once.

"Hee hee whoooo, hee hee whoooo."

Maybe breathing like a woman about to give birth will help. Is this even how they breathe?

Ben's brows crease in confusion as he listens to my ridiculous attempt at breathing through the pain.

"Should I take you to the hospital?"

"Spicy…ahhhh."

I can't even answer his question properly because I'm attacked by another round of agonizing cramps. My hands clench around the leather as I lift my butt slightly off the seat in a futile attempt to ease the onslaught.

And that's when it happens.

I'm struck by the awful realization that I'm about to pass wind and there is absolutely nothing I can do about it, no matter how hard I clench my butt cheeks together. All I can do now is pray that nothing more than gas comes out. Even though it feels like I'm dying, I might *actually* die of shame if that happens.

I've seen it when I played the *Sims*. You can literally die of shame. It's a thing.

"I'm so sorry." I whisper the words as a tear rolls down my cheek.

I just want to crawl into a hole and disappear. Ben will probably never want to see me again after tonight.

The confusion on Ben's face turns to alarm as I let rip with the loudest fart ever known to man.

Mum has always *hated* that word. Vulgar, she says. I could say I tooted, fluffed, broke wind, butt-burped, experienced an unusual amount of flatulence, or my mum's favorite: exhaled from my rear, but those would be far too tame descriptions for what just happened. The entire car seems to vibrate with the fury of that flatulence. It is a moment that will forever be seared into my memory.

And probably Ben's.

And the smell. Oh heavens above, *the smell*. My nostrils are under attack by a putrid hot cloud of death and decay.

When I see Ben holding his breath and frantically stabbing at buttons to lower the windows, my lone tear becomes a cascade. My body is convulsing and I'm not really sure if it's from the relentless bowel tantrums or from the sobs that I can't seem to get under control.

I'm trying to control my abject crying while simultaneously

dealing with cramps, and trying desperately to make sure nothing else leaks out. It's too much. It's all too much!

I've never been more mortified in my life, and I've done a fair number of embarrassing things. Like that time I said, "Hey, little man" to somebody I thought was a co-worker's kid—turned out it was a new client who was just a really short bloke with a genetic disorder. In my defense, it was "bring your kid to work" day. Or the time I fell asleep on a stranger's shoulder on a long flight and drooled all over his shirt. Or the split trousers incident of 2019. But nothing compares to this moment.

My door opens before the car has even come to a full stop.

Ben shouts something but I can't hear what he says.

"Sorry. Thanks. I'll call," I shout over my shoulder as I race up the stairs to my new apartment building, clutching my stomach.

I'm not sure how true that is. I don't know if I can ever face Ben again. My cheeks get hot at even the thought of it.

The poor guy just had his fancy car engulfed in a cloud that smelled like decomposing rodent flesh. He's probably, at the minute, telling his friends all about this crazy British girl who farted in his posh car and they'll all be having a laugh about it.

I spend a ridiculously long time in the bathroom, thinking about how this incident has quite possibly trampled my friendship with Ben into oblivion. The only silver lining is that Ben isn't here to witness the unholy noises I'm making while the world falls out of my butt.

Finally, the cramps ease. I don't think there could possibly be anything left to come out of my body.

I have a quick shower because that's all my weak body can manage before I stumble into bed and give in to the exhaustion.

CHAPTER FOURTEEN

I ROLL out of bed on Saturday morning and hobble to the kitchen. After about five trips to the bathroom during the night, I'm feeling washed out.

A glance in the mirror at my wild hair and baggy sweats only confirms my fears. I look like a homeless person. Just call me "Hobo Kate".

I'm never eating spicy food again.

My sluggish steps come to an abrupt halt when I spot a note on the counter, along with a bottle of Gatorade, a pack of Imodium, and some Trioral rehydration sachets.

Knocked by there was no answer. Door was unlocked.

I went and picked up a few things because I wasn't sure you'd have anything in your new apartment.

I'll lock up when I leave and push the key under the door.

Hope you sleep okay. Call me if you need anything else.

Feel better soon.

Ben

It's good to know that he hasn't been completely repulsed by my lack of sphincter control. And thank goodness he locked the door. The idea of sleeping with my apartment door unlocked in a mostly empty building gives me chills, but it's not like security was uppermost in my thoughts while my bowels were wringing themselves dry.

After rehydrating and eating some toast with Marmite I feel so much better. I make a mental note to add Marmite to the list of things Mum and Dad need to bring when they visit. And some tea cakes.

The buzzing of my phone on the counter pulls me from my thoughts of all things British.

"So, how was it then? I couldn't wait until brunch tomorrow. I'm dying to find out," Clem asks.

"Hello to you too," I reply drily. "It ended in tears."

"Really? What did he do?" I can hear the suspicion in her voice. "Do I need to sic Dan on him?"

"Not *mine*. His. Well, mine came later, but that's another story entirely."

"Wait, *he* was the one crying?"

"Yes, because apparently, he's in love with somebody he can never have—his sister-in-law." I could go into a bit more detail but I'm waiting for the screech of disbelief on the other end.

Clementine doesn't disappoint. Although I'm not sure if the underlying emotion is disbelief or glee. You can tell our mums are sisters. She definitely got some of the family genes in the drama department.

"Good gracious!"

"I know, but you can't help but feel sorry for the chap. He's actually really sweet. We can't always help who we fall in love with and it's not like he can just distance himself very easily. It's family."

"How did that topic even come up?"

"Well, I asked him what made him decide to try online dating and it all just came spilling out. It was like a dam wall burst."

"So, that explains *his* tears. How did *you* end up crying?"

I spill the details to Clem, in all their horrifying glory. Thinking about the most embarrassing moment of my life just makes me want to die of shame all over again. I contemplate hanging up because she's laughing so hard that I can hear her wheezing. She sounds like our ninety-year-old nan with emphysema.

When she finally gets herself under control enough to speak, her words are a mirror of my own thoughts.

"Wonder what Ben thinks of you now?" I can hear she's trying hard not to start laughing again. "I suppose it can't be that bad if he brought you medication. If he didn't want to see you again, he definitely wouldn't have done that."

She makes a good point, but I'm too tired and weak to think about what this means.

"He may not take you in his posh car again though," Clem jokes, which sets off another round of cackling for her. I can tell she's going to get a lot of comedy mileage out of this incident.

"Clem, if you tell your mum what happened, I'm disowning you. Aunty Dot will get straight on the phone to my mother and I'll never hear the end of it. When she gets over the second-hand embarrassment, she'll find it hysterical. She'll be telling her grandbabies about this one day."

"It'll go in the vault, I promise," she manages to reply after regaining her composure.

After Clem promises to drop off soup for me later, I climb back into bed and dream of handsome bartenders.

***

"Hey Kate, are you feeling okay? You look pretty pale."

Viola looks at me with a small frown etched on her perfect face as she sets up her desk for the day. She looks like she just stepped out of the pages of a fashion magazine in her sunshine yellow dress that hugs her in all the right places and shows off her toned legs. The second week of work here, one of my celebrity clients came to the office and caught a glimpse of Viola. He's been hounding me about whether she's single ever since.

For a change, I keep my lips firmly zipped. There is no way I'm filling anybody in on what happened this weekend. I'd never live it down. The little French blabbermouth would probably share the news with the entire office before the end of the day.

I glance over in the direction of Alex's desk and am not surprised to see the nosy parker peering over our shared partition.

"I'm fine thank you, Viola. I wasn't feeling very well this

weekend, but I'm better now."

Aside from a brief phone call with Clem, and a less brief phone call with my mum and dad, I basically slept the entire weekend.

It took a good while to convince my mum that it was just spicy food and my intestines playing games, and not a date that had tried to poison me. Of course, I didn't give her any of the humiliating details about the ride home. I only told her about the upset tummy. She was, however, enthralled by the story of poor Carter and no doubt phoned Aunty Dot straight after our call.

"So 'ow was your date? The football player, yes?"

"He was very sweet, but not really my type."

I'm not giving him any of those details either. It's one thing to tell my mum, who is an ocean away. It's an entirely different thing to tell the office gossip who'll only spread the news. What if somebody at work actually knows the guy? That would be terrible, and for some reason I feel a sense of loyalty to Carter the quarterback, poor bloke.

Alex laughs and then raises an eyebrow at me. "Football player is everybody's type. I saw the photo."

It was a great photo. He stares off into space for a minute. Just when I think I've managed to escape his interrogation, he comes back to reality and narrows his eyes at me.

"Something must 'ave 'appened on the date! So, what was it?"

He rests his chin on his hands and waits for a response. I'm about to tell him it's none of his beeswax when Viola swoops in and saves me.

"How about you tell us about *your* date on Saturday instead, Alex? You two looked pretty cozy when I bumped into you."

In a flash, Alex's surprised face disappears from view as he sits back down. The movement is quickly followed by the rhythmic ticking of the keyboard as he gets back to work.

I'm just as surprised as he is by this statement.

Catching Viola's attention, I mouth, "Date?"

She simply winks at me before spinning around on her chair and getting down to business.

At the end of the day as I begin packing up my things, a text pings on my phone. It's Ben. This is the first contact I've had with him since my very brief thank you message.

BEN: Hey. Are you feeling better?
KATE: Yes. Thanks again.

BEN: Anytime. We still on for game night on Wednesday?

I don't know whether I should feel relieved or embarrassed by the fact that he seems to be pretending like nothing ever happened. He basically smelled death and he's carrying on like normal.

The only thing that gives me a small modicum of comfort is the fact that it could have been worse. It could have been more than just wind that I passed. Small mercies.

KATE: Sure. And yes, I haven't forgotten that you get to pick the movie.
BEN: I'll also pick up some food, but don't worry, nothing spicy *wink*

Okay, so he's not completely ignoring my most embarrassing moment ever, but at least he has a sense of humor about it. He even used a wink emoji. *Cute.*

Before I have a chance to reply there are more pings.

BEN: What dates have you got lined up this week?
BEN: Jackson got tickets to a comedy show on Thursday if you're interested.
KATE: I'd love that. Thanks. Only got a date on Friday night.
BEN: Great. We can discuss the details when I see you on Wednesday.

I'm excited about meeting more of Ben's friends. If Boston is going to be home for the foreseeable future, I need to expand my social circle. Aside from my co-workers, Ben is really my only friend.

***

I press the buzzer to Ben's apartment with a little bit of trepidation. It's our Wednesday night game night and this is the first time I've seen him since *the incident*.

He doesn't seem to be too bothered about it, because he's been texting me as normal the entire week, so as much as a part of me wants to crawl in a hole and disappear, I know I need to bite the bullet and face the man.

"Come on up."

As I reach the landing at the top, his door swings open and he greets me with a huge smile.

"You made it. I wasn't sure if I'd need to carry you again."

"Ha! No racquetball for me this time, and I've recovered from the weekend."

"I'm glad to hear it. I was worried about you," he says quietly, engulfing me in a hug.

There is still a part of me that is utterly mortified by what happened, but an even bigger part of me is relieved that Ben is being so normal. I was worried I'd ruined things forever.

Instead of ordering out, Ben has cooked a light dinner himself. I'm not quite sure what it is, all I know is it's some crockpot chicken dish, like some kind of broth. Served with freshly baked bread (which he proudly told me he made himself), it makes a delicious meal.

I'm really touched that he would go to all that effort for me. He's so thoughtful.

I don't know why he doesn't want a serious relationship because he'd be so good at it. He's a natural. He's caring, thoughtful, and if the last few days have taught me anything, it's that he's empathetic and goes out of his way to help people. He's a real catch.

But I can't dwell on that thought too much because it's just depressing to think about. Here is the perfect guy and he is unattainable. He is everything I want in a husband, except for the rather large issue of not wanting to settle down.

Instead, I should be focusing on how fortunate I am to have met Ben. Even if he's not the one, he's the most amazing friend a girl could ask for.

And a little bit of eye-candy in friends never hurt anyone, right?

Well, that's what I tell myself anyway, as I watch Ben's perfect butt as he heads back to the kitchen to rinse our dirty dishes.

After I've helped him pack the dishwasher, we make ourselves comfortable on the floor in front of the television.

"So, what are we playing tonight? More Mario Kart?"

"No. I love Mario Kart, but variety is the spice of life so I thought we could try something different. We're playing *Overcooked*. I think we should save the movie for another night though. Don't want you falling asleep and drooling all over my couch again."

He's cheeky, but I chuckle, because I know that under the teasing jab the real reason for not wanting to watch a movie afterwards is because he wants me to get home safely at a reasonable hour.

After loading the game, he hands me a controller.

"May the best chef win!"

CHAPTER FIFTEEN

"MR. AND Mrs. Walsh came home early and caught us setting off fireworks on the roof. They were *not* happy. They were even less happy the next time it rained and they discovered just how much damage fireworks could do to a roof. Although, that still doesn't compare to how mad Mammy Walsh got the time we used her antique quilt to make a fort in the forest behind Ben's house. It was a family heirloom."

Ben rolls his eyes as I chuckle at the story.

We're at a cute Italian place just a short walk from the comedy club with five of Ben's friends.

His best friend, Will, has had me in stitches with stories from Ben's childhood. They grew up together on the Vineyard.

He's easy going and I can see why he and Ben are such good friends. He also has a sexy lumberjack vibe going on with his full beard and plaid shirt. I'm sure the ladies love him.

Jackson, I've already met. As for Claire, Natalie, and Caleb, it's quite difficult to get a read on them because they've spent almost the entire dinner grilling me with more questions than a CIA interrogation.

"So Kate, Ben told us you're trying out some online dating. How's that going?" Claire asks me while we're eating dinner.

I give a very unladylike snort before answering Claire.

"Well, let's see…I've had dates with an extreme germaphobe, a guy with a friends-with-benefits he won't give up, a guy still in love with his ex, a guy in love with his sister-in-law, and an almost-date with somebody who had a very disturbing fetish. I think I should write a book: *The Dating Misadventures of Kate Callahan*. I think it's safe to say I'm not doing so well at this online dating thing."

"Aw, don't give up yet! I know a few couples who met online and now they're married. It's *so* romantic." Natalie's eyes glaze over as she sighs, resting her chin on her hand.

"It's dangerous if you ask me. Aren't you worried you're going to end up with some psycho?" Caleb asks.

Before I have a chance to answer him, Claire chimes in.

"I'd be worried. There are a lot of crazy people out there. If you ask me, the best way to meet people when you're new to a city is through friends. You know, I've had a pretty successful track record in setting friends up. I like to think of myself as a bit of a Love Guru."

She gives Will and Natalie a pointed look.

"I'm not sure one couple counts as a 'track record'," Will says with a smirk as he puts his arm around Natalie and steals a slice of pizza from her plate.

"Oh shush. You guys are not the only couple I set up. It's also thanks to my matchmaking skills and a little subterfuge that my boss is now dating one of our suppliers. I have a nose for these things. Now Kate, I know a great guy named Jason I used to work with. You remember Jason, Ben? You guys met at the pub quiz? Anyway, he's single at the moment and you guys would be perfect for each other! He's away at the moment, but I'll talk to him as soon as he gets back."

Ben doesn't respond, but Claire looks so excited about the idea that I can't help but smile at her enthusiasm.

"Yeah, maybe."

"We'd better get going if we don't want to be late," Ben says, looking a little bit uncomfortable.

As everybody stands and gathers their things I sneak a look at Ben. He looks pensive.

"Everything okay?" I ask quietly as we head out the door and make our way to the comedy club.

"Yeah, everything's fine."

Ben gives me a tight smile that doesn't reach his eyes. It doesn't reassure me at all, but I feel slightly better when he places his hand on my lower back, steering me through the rather crowded sidewalk outside the venue.

***

My date, Marco, is thirty minutes late. I'm back at The Old Copper Pig for my Friday date, and tap my fingers on the table in an impatient rhythm.

To his credit, he did send me a text about fifteen minutes ago saying he was on his way.

I haven't even been able to chat to Ben because he's not working tonight.

"How are you doing? Can I get you another Coke?"

I look up at the waiter. "No thanks. Hopefully my date will be here soon."

"Okay. Let me know if you change your mind. I promised Ben I'd look after you."

Ben asked somebody to look out for me? Interesting. I'll file that information away for later.

Before I can respond, my date saunters through the door. It's the cocky swagger of somebody who has no confidence issues. Maybe a bit too self-assured. I'm not sure if I like this.

Mercifully, he looks just like his profile picture.

Marco runs a hand through his thick dark hair as he scans the restaurant, giving me time to appreciate the view. He's tall, dark, and handsome, so I suppose looks-wise, we're off to a good start.

Just then, he spots me and gives a friendly wave before making his way over.

"Hi, Kate? I'm so sorry I'm late," he says and takes his seat. "My mother locked herself out of her house."

"Oh no! I'm sorry."

I don't really know why I'm apologizing. I realized it must be a British thing when Ben pointed out how often I do it. I hadn't even realized. It's not just an apology. It's being polite. It's for sympathy. Apparently when you're British, there's no such thing as overusing the word "sorry".

As much as I abhor lateness, at least Marco has a good reason for being late so I can't really hold it against him. I do love a man who treats his mother well.

"Well, it's not the first time it's happened." He laughs. "After the third time, I just made a copy of her key."

He smiles at me and I can't help but notice how brilliantly white and straight his teeth are. I'm talking blindingly white. He could be in toothpaste commercials.

"So how did a guy like you end up on a dating app?" I ask.

One of the first things I notice when he answers my question is that he talks with his hands. Marco's very animated. And very funny. He has a great sense of humor but going by my track record, I don't want to count my chickens just yet.

The only teeny, tiny red flag is that whenever I ask him about his job, Marco gives vague non-answers and changes the topic. *Strange.*

His profile says he's a hedge fund manager, so I can't quite work out why he's so reluctant to discuss it. It's not like the guy is in the CIA or anything.

The other small thing that starts to grate on my nerves is that he sniffs and rubs his nose regularly.

I realize this makes me a total hypocrite because my allergies are sometimes completely out of control. Especially around cats. But I'm sure I don't sniff as much as he does, even on bad days.

At least Marco fits the list. He has a stable job (even if he won't talk about it), a great sense of humor, is looking for something serious, and he's attractive.

Another big plus is that conversation flows very easily. He's clearly a people-person.

"Not anything for me, thanks," Marco politely declines when the dessert menu is offered. "I have an eating plan I'm trying to stick to."

By the looks of his sculpted chest and arms, his dedication to it is clearly paying off.

I wish I could say I had that same determination, but I don't. Not even close. I like cheeseburgers and pizza, and all the other good things.

As much as I would love to try the fudge sundae Ben told me about, I can't just eat dessert while my date watches. That would be awkward. Instead, I just ask for the cheque.

He doesn't offer to pay for the meal, but I'm absolutely fine with splitting the bill.

When the date ends, Marco walks me to my car like a gentleman, gives me a chaste kiss on the cheek and says he'll call me. For a change, it wasn't a bad date.

I really shouldn't be so judgmental about the sniffing. Nobody's perfect. Perhaps he's feeling a bit under the weather. And as for the job, maybe when we get to know each other better, he'll talk about it.

Perhaps this internet dating thing will work out after all.

***

I'm just getting down to work on Monday morning when my phone pings with a text message.

MARCO: Thx 4 Friday. Was awesome. Want to take u out Saturday but my car is in the shop. $$$$$

I can totally empathize. Thankfully the mechanic Ben called didn't charge a lot to fix my car, but it's still an unexpected expense. I tap out a quick response. Just as I put my phone on my desk, it pings again.

MARCO: Can u lend me $500? I'll pay u back. U know I'm good 4 it. U can Venmo it.

Alex, who's just swanned into the office, clocks the expression on my face and asks, "What is it?"

I turn the phone towards him and reply, "Friday's blind date. Marco the hedge fund manager."

At that, Viola spins around on her chair, her eyes wide. "Did you just say a hedge fund manager named Marco?"

"Yes." I'm still preoccupied with the text. "Why on earth would a hedge fund manager need to borrow money? I thought they were rolling in it."

I'm utterly confused by this turn of events.

"Um…" Viola looks awkward. "Can I see his profile picture?"

"Sure." I open up the app on my phone and pull up Marco's profile. As I do, I hear a gasp from Viola.

"Oh no!"

"What? What is it? She knows 'im!" Alex is suddenly very invested in this conversation. His hands are flapping about in excitement.

"Oh honey." Viola rubs my arm sympathetically. "Last Saturday I went out with my friend, Winnie, to that new club near Royale.

Anyway, turns out the DJ that night was none other than Marco, her blind date from the week before, who had told her he was a hedge fund manager. Not only is he most definitely *not* a hedge fund manager, but we found out from the bartender who overheard us talking about him that he also has a girlfriend."

"No!" Alex voices what I'm thinking.

Once again, my mouth is agape. If I had a dollar for every time I'd done that since I started with this online dating nonsense I'd be able to retire early.

"That's not all, Kate. The bartender also said his nickname was Marco the Narco because he has a bit of a narcotics problem." She taps her nose as she says this. "He's bad news Kate."

This is terrible news. I finally thought I'd found a good one. No wonder he couldn't stop sniffing!

"So, I guess 'e only wants your money for a bit of the devil's dandruff," Alex chimes in.

"Firstly, eeeew! Secondly, I don't need a reminder of how much my dating life sucks."

I drop my head to my desk in despair. Maybe I'm going about this all wrong. I mean, how can one person possibly experience so many dating disasters? Is my luck really that bad? Never mind Mr. Right, I can't even find a Mr. Okay. I suppose I should be grateful I found all this out now. Being with no one is better than being with the wrong one.

"Oh Kate, I'm sorry. You'll find the right person. I know you will. You're a total catch. I told you a couple of my clients have asked if you're single. I could always set you up with one of them." Viola tries her best to cheer me up, but her pep talk is interrupted by her phone ringing. She glances at the screen and rolls her eyes.

"You did something this weekend that I'm going to have to fix, didn't you?" Our sweet Viola doesn't even bother with a greeting, and that's how Alex and I both know straight away who it is.

Although her phone isn't on speaker, the volume is loud enough for us to hear Noah King's gruff voice on the other end of the line, confirming our suspicions.

"I don't see why it's a big deal."

He knows just how to push darling Viola's buttons. We don't hear the rest of his response because she's already walking away, but we do catch her salty reply.

"Noah, I don't have the patience or the crayons to explain this to you…"

I head to the break room with my lunch and think about Viola's comment. The one client who asked about my relationship status was a hockey player, and the other an actor. I'm not so sure I like the idea of going on a blind date with either of them.

Working in this industry has taught me that a lot of people who hire PR companies to manage their reputation, are pretty arrogant. They're celebrities and they know it. They're used to people fawning all over them. There are exceptions, of course. Most of my clients are wonderful, but dating a client of the company? I don't know if that's such a great idea. Things could get pretty awkward if it doesn't work out. I wouldn't want to be married to a celebrity anyway, so it seems a pretty pointless exercise.

Just as I'm sitting down to eat my salad, my phone dances across the table in the breakroom as it blasts Mum's ringtone.

We never got to have our regular Sunday afternoon call because they were away for the weekend.

"Hello Mum."

"Darling! It's so lovely to hear your voice. Feels like it's been ages."

"Mum, we spoke last Sunday."

"That's too long ago. Eight days! Maybe we should make our calls twice a week."

Oh good heavens no! I love my mum, I really do, but she is a lot. Once a week is just perfect. I decide to quickly change the subject before she gets any more crazy ideas.

"So how was your weekend? How is Nan?"

Mission accomplished. Mum's peeling laughter rings through the phone and I give myself a mental fist pump for distracting her so well.

"Well apparently Nan and Edna got into an argument that turned into a brawl this week. Something about Edna taking too many napkins at lunch."

"A brawl! Over napkins?" I'm shocked. Although I probably shouldn't be. Nan may be ninety, but she's a feisty old thing.

"Well, it started out over napkins, but you know Nan. Edna wasn't having it and shook her fist at Nan saying, 'Things are about to get real Margaret', and then Nan said 'Oh yeah? Real like your hips? Or your teeth?' and then there was some hair-pulling and screaming. Dentures fell out. The nurses and security had to pull them apart. Now they're banned from being in the same room together for the foreseeable future."

"Good gracious!"

"Poor Arthur is also in Nan's bad books. She accused him of cheating at bingo. It's not his fault he can't see the numbers properly. The poor old chap is as blind as a bat. He couldn't cheat, even if he wanted to."

"Nan really needs to tone it down, Mum. One day she's going to get into some real trouble with that mouth of hers. You're going to have coppers knocking on your door and you're going to have to bail her out of the slammer."

"The slammer? Really, Catherine! These Americans are rubbing off on you. Anyway, darling, how was your weekend? How was your blind date?"

I knew that was the real reason Mum had called. For all her objections over online dating, she is well and truly invested in the process.

"The date itself was fine, but then he messaged this morning asking for money."

There's no way I'm telling Mum about his little drug problem. Although she loves the juicy gossip, she's still worried I'm going to meet a rapist or serial killer, and this won't help the cause.

"What a cheek! Sounds like that lazy Johnny you used to date. Awful chap, always asking for money like some leech. He even tried to scrounge off me and your father! I was so happy when you broke up with him. I always thought he was a few sandwiches short of a picnic, dear."

"Well then you'll be thrilled to know I don't plan to see this guy again."

"Good for you, darling. Don't lower your standards."

I definitely won't be doing that. The checklist is there for a reason…even if it is proving impossible to find Mr. Perfect.

"Where's Dad? I've got to get back to work but I want to say a quick hello."

"Oh, he's in the garden. He's been there all day. The new peonies arrived bright and early. I'll call him."

"Don't worry, Mum. His hands are probably covered in dirt. I need to get back to work anyway."

I wouldn't tear Dad away from his gardening. He loves pottering around the garden and his greenhouse.

"Ok, darling. I'll tell him you say hello. Love you. Kisses."
"I love you too, Mum. Bye."

CHAPTER SIXTEEN

"YOU TOOK these yourself?"

Ben is looking at the framed photographs I've hung on the walls. The only thing I've added to the already-furnished apartment. He sounds surprised.

"Yeah. I love crumbled and abandoned buildings. There's something I find beautiful about the decay and erosion of weathered stone and bricks."

"I know what you mean," Ben replies, still looking reverently at the photographs. "It's like every crack and crevice whispers secrets of a bygone place."

"Wow, Ben. That was…poetic."

He gets it. It's just a hobby, but it's important to me. The fact that he seems to appreciate the haunting allure of these crumbled sites as much as I do is…surprising. In the best way. The thought makes my heart do funny things in my chest.

I need to change the subject before I dwell too much on that.

"Don't worry, I haven't forgotten that you get to choose the movie. So, what are we watching then? *Mission Impossible? The Fast and the Furious?*" I ask.

Ben has come over for our first official Monday Movie Night. After I fell asleep at his place, we decided it was better to split up the game and movie night so that we're not awake until all hours of the morning on a week day. Very responsible and adult of us.

Ben turns to look at me with a big grin on his face.

"*Gilmore Girls*!" he announces proudly.

I couldn't possibly have heard that correctly. The night of the NSBSD (*NOT silent, but STILL deadly*) incident when Ben gave me a ride and I'd promised he could pick the movie, I'd assumed it would be some action movie.

"Did you just say *Gilmore Girls*?"

"Yes."

"As in the TV series? *Gilmore Girls*?"

"Yes."

"*Gilmore Girls*?" I know I'm repeating myself like a stuck record, but I can't help it.

"Have a bit of a hearing problem there, Callahan?" Ben raises an eyebrow.

"No. I just…I don't know. I've got to be honest, you don't really strike me as the type to like *Gilmore Girls*. You seem more of a *Top Gun* kind of guy."

"Oh I am. I love *Top Gun*. But what's not to love about *Gilmore Girls*?"

He's dead serious and that makes me laugh. He so utterly adorable I could squish him.

"So we're watching *A Year in the Life* movie?"

"No, we're watching the series. From season one," he says with absolute seriousness as he settles down on my couch and points the remote at the television.

I can't stop laughing.

"But it's Monday *Movie* Night. That's not a movie. This is going to take ages to get through. It'll be months before I get to choose a movie! That's cheating."

"We should change the name then. Monday Series Night. Doesn't quite have the same ring to it, does it? Maybe just *Gilmore Girls* Night. And it's not cheating, it's…bending the rules." He pauses his clicking of the remote to look at me. "Do you have something against Lorelai and Rory?"

That sets off the giggles again and I have to bite my lip to get them under control.

"No, not at all. I actually love *Gilmore Girls*. I just can't believe you do too. I've never met a guy who enjoys it. It seems, I don't know, a bit of a girly show maybe?"

"Well then it's a good thing I'm confident enough in my masculinity to not worry about things like that," he says with a grin and gives me a little nudge with his elbow. "Come on, get comfortable. We've got seven seasons to get through."

***

With the phone to my ear, I drum my fingers impatiently on the desk, waiting to get a word in. I'm only half-listening. I'm mainly thinking about how immensely grateful I am for our new plan of splitting up game and movie night.

This new plan ensured I got plenty of sleep. And boy did I need it because all hell broke loose when I arrived at work this morning, thanks to an unruly celebrity couple that I'm unfortunate enough to call clients.

I love my job and I adore my clients. Most of them. But these two actors are the bane of my existence, and if I could offload them on another publicist, I would. They are A-listers who believe the world revolves around them and refuse to take my advice, but get upset when their actions land them in trouble.

I'm still not sure why they bother to employ a PR company when they maintain absolute control over everything that happens, and ignore all our advice. At least, the wife does, and the husband does pretty much whatever his wife tells him to.

Last night, an interview aired—an interview that I vehemently advised them against participating in because I knew exactly how it would turn out. As their publicist, I should have watched it instead of happily devouring episodes of *Gilmore Girls*.

I have no regrets.

The problem is that their statements have been fact-checked and many of them have proved to be false, as I knew they would, because, like most celebrities, they love to twist a story to suit their own narrative. They act impulsively, and assume that because they're famous everybody will buy the tall tale they're trying to sell. Now they're the laughing stock of Hollywood (which is not a good thing when you're an actor) and they want me to fix it.

This is how I find myself on an hour-long phone call to LA on Tuesday afternoon. I restlessly drum my fingers on my desk while I wait for a chance to speak. I'm losing patience fast.

"I understand, but as I explained to you before, going on the offensive all the time is not a good look for you. You may feel justified in your attacks but..."

I don't get to finish and have to hold the phone away from my ear because of the tongue lashing I'm getting. Alex is, as usual, peeking over the partition and keeping track of what's going on. Not that he really needs to. I'm sure half the office can hear her high-pitched screeching without much effort. It didn't help that one of the many celebrities they slandered in the interview is another client of ours. They also didn't have very pleasant things to say about fans, their families, the press…pretty much everybody else in the world is the problem.

"Yes, I realize *you* don't think it's an attack, it's just *your truth*…" I can't help but roll my eyes, which makes Alex chuckle. Thank goodness my clients are not here in the flesh to see me. "…but the rest of the world *perceives* it as an attack. And as we discussed before, when the world is starving and at war, they don't want to hear celebrities attack people and complain about how hard their lives are. It's not relatable. It comes across as bitter and self-centered. I'm telling you again, you need to completely rebrand yourselves."

After listening to another speech of how useless I am, I finally manage to end the call. I put my head in my hands and let out a long, exhausted breath.

"Did you see the latest 'eadline and comments?" Alex asks. "The world thinks they need to fire Pied Piper because this interview was a terrible idea. *Tu te fous de moi?* As if our clients always listen to us!"

That's the problem. They refuse to listen to sense. I don't know why they bother to hire publicists when they do their own thing anyway.

They're rude and obnoxious, and speak down to everybody else, but they also pay Pied Piper a small fortune in fees, so there's no way the boss is going to dump them.

Just then my phone vibrates on my desk.

BEN: How's my favorite publicist?
KATE: I'm pretty sure I'm the only publicist you know.
BEN: Semantics. How's your day going?
KATE: Today has been a three-ring circus without the entertainment. I need to cancel our Wednesday night game night.
BEN: No! *sad face emoji*
KATE: Blame the celebrity couple I was telling you about. I have to fly to LA tomorrow to kick their butts.

BEN: Butt kicking sounds fun.

KATE: I'm sure it is. If only I could really do it. I'm actually going to try calm them down and get them to agree to a new PR strategy.

BEN: Sounds painful.

KATE: Wish me luck.

BEN: You're amazing. If anybody can do it you can. You rock!

A ribbon of warmth coils around my heart at his words.

KATE: Can I hire you as my personal cheerleader?

BEN: I mean every word. Text me when you get there so I know you're safe.

KATE: I'll text you when I get back too, just so you know they didn't murder me.

My fingers dance across the screen as I type out a quick response to Ben's latest text. The moment I hit send, a familiar zing of excitement courses through my veins, making my heart flutter with anticipation.

Texting with Ben always has a way of electrifying my mood, filling each conversation with a delightful energy that I can't resist. It's a playful dance of words that leaves me grinning after every exchange. Messaging Ben has become one of my favorite things to do. It's a source of joy, a little dose of exhilaration that never fails to brighten even the most miserable day.

You need to get this crush under control, Catherine.

Even my conscience is resorting to my full name in a scolding that makes no difference whatsoever. My traitorous heart won't seem to get the memo that Ben is off limits.

***

There isn't much time to think about Ben.

What is supposed to be a one-night visit to Los Angeles, turns into a two-night visit. That's how long it takes to stop the tantrum these two are throwing. They are beyond furious that they're getting so much bad publicity for their interview.

On a few occasions I've looked at the wife's screaming red face and wondered if it might actually explode. Maybe this is how spontaneous human combustion happens—another thing Mum's read all about. I've never seen rage like this before. She threw plates! Actual dinner plates! Clear across the kitchen. My text to Ben about being murdered doesn't seem too far-fetched now.

There may not be *much* time to think about him, but that doesn't mean I don't.

Do I think about him every spare moment I have, and even some moments where I should be thinking about work? Why yes. Yes, I do.

By the time I get back to Boston on Friday, I'm utterly exhausted. It doesn't help that trying to drum up some positive PR to drown out the negative is proving challenging. My clients are convinced the solution is to buy a few humanitarian awards…which, believe it or not, is actually possible. They've done it once before behind my back. I'm trying to convince them that the backlash will be even worse if they do that and the truth comes out. More subtle, positive PR (that is *actually* true) is a much better strategy.

Their shenanigans are draining the life out of me, so the last thing I want to do is go on a blind date tonight. I haven't even been home yet, but I don't want to cancel at the last minute.

I've been cursed at more these last few days than I have in my entire life. I wouldn't be surprised if the wife buys a little voodoo doll and starts sticking pins in it. She really is that venomous.

Give me rappers trying to sneak llamas into the country over this insufferable pair any day!

CHAPTER SEVENTEEN

AS USUAL, The Old Copper Pig is bustling on Friday night.

I hear my name as soon as I walk through the doors. "Kate?"

My date for the evening, Patrick, is leaning against the bar. Just behind him I catch a glimpse of Ben, who makes a face.

Okay, so Ben definitely doesn't like the guy.

Not a great start, especially after the week I've had.

Patrick grips me by the elbow and leads me to a table. I'm immediately on my guard and it's not because of Ben's reaction. There's something about the way that Patrick grips my elbow that I don't like. It's not painful, but it's not a gentle touch either. It's a bit too firm and forceful for my liking.

I glance back at the bar and am pleased to see Ben has got his eyes glued to the table. It makes me feel a lot better, knowing that he's watching because something about this guy just feels…*off.*

"Tell me about yourself Katie. What do you like doing for fun?" Patrick laces his fingers together and leans far back in his chair while we wait for our food.

This feels a bit like an interview.

"It's just Kate. Well, I like to read. I like cooking. I also dabble in a little bit of photography. I like taking photos of abandoned, crumbling buildings. There's something beautiful about the decay."

"Sounds like a weird hobby. You should photograph people instead. That's more normal," Patrick tells me, with a slight sneer.

It's impossible not to contrast his reaction to the one I got from

Ben. Before he left on Monday night, he took another look at the photographs hanging on my walls. He was speechless. He said they were beautiful and even asked for copies. Patrick just thinks it's a weird hobby.

"Well, what do you like to do?"

"I like weapons. I collect lots of different weapons. Guns, knives, crossbows, swords, axes. I have an axe so sharp it could slice a man clean through. I'd love to show you sometime."

Uh. No thanks?

And he thinks taking photos of abandoned buildings is weird? It's not the weapons I have a problem with, per se. I have a good friend who has his own forge and crafts his own knives. They're beautiful. Truly. It's artistry. But I can't shake this feeling in my gut that there is something off about this guy.

I'm momentarily distracted from these disturbing thoughts by the arrival of our food. I think it came in record time.

As I tuck into the delicious meal I steal a glance at Ben. I'm thrilled to see that not only does he still have his eyes glued to our table, but he's actually moved around to the other side of the bar and is sitting on one of the stools with his arms folded, facing us. He's not being subtle about his observation.

When Ben winks at me I think I might melt into a puddle in my chair.

Be still my heart.

Although truthfully, I don't know if it's racing because of Ben or because creepy Patrick has me on edge.

The state of my nerves does not improve when Patrick starts talking about his ex-girlfriend. Apparently she was a gold-digger, and a few other choice words that my mum would have a heart attack hearing. His language is absolutely vulgar. Really, no woman should be called those things.

"So, did it end badly?"

"Well, for *her* it did!" Patrick laughs mildly and before I can ask what that cryptic remark meant, he adds, "She was killed in an accident."

My brain is trying to catch up with what's happening. I was referring to the end of their relationship. Why would he laugh about her dying in an accident? That's horrible. Is he really so cold-hearted?

"That's very sad. I'm so sorry. Was it a car accident?"

Patrick gives me a look that pierces right through me. His eyes are an icy blue. Normally, I would think they're a beautiful color, but they seem devoid of any life or warmth. They are cold. Soulless. His unsettling gaze feels like a predator sizing up its prey.

That's me! I'm the prey!

What was I thinking? Blind dates are a terrible idea!

Despite my best efforts to brush it off as mere nerves, I can't shake the eerie feeling that something sinister lurks behind his piercing eyes.

After a painfully long silence, Patrick finally answers.

"No. It was a *different* kind of accident."

His words send an icy current coursing through my veins, urging me to retreat. He's totally giving off sinister vibes and it's sending alarm bells clanging through me.

I send a slightly panicked look in Ben's direction and he immediately gets up from his stool with a questioning look on his face. I think he's trying to work out if I want to be rescued or if I can handle this myself.

As Patrick starts talking about his love of horror movies, I look down at our half-eaten meals, wondering how to politely extract myself from this situation without angering him. I don't want to get on the bad side of a guy who has a massive collection of weapons and potentially is a psychopath.

Just then, I notice a little ant wandering across the table. Actually, it's rather large for an ant. It looks like a carpenter ant. I'd better tell Ben they should check their wood in case there's an infestation.

The next few moments are a blur as everything seems to happen at once. While I'm watching, I suddenly see a blade slice the ant in two and then my body is being yanked up. It takes me a few seconds to register that Patrick has whipped out a switchblade mid-conversation and carved the ant up, just as Ben hauled me out of my chair.

My brain is overloaded. My heart is galloping so fast I'm sure everybody can hear it. Patrick brought a knife to our date! The thought terrifies me. Ben, bless him, looks as cool as a cucumber even though I can feel a slight tremor in the hand that's on my back.

"Are you Kate? There's an emergency call for you."

That's so odd. Why is Ben asking if I'm Kate? And who would be calling me here? What emergency?

My slow brain only manages to catch up to Ben's smooth extraction as he hands me over to a waiter before turning his attention to Patrick.

As the waiter is leading me towards a door marked "staff only", I crane my neck to see what's happening, catching Ben's words.

"I'm afraid I'm going to have to ask you to leave, sir. We don't allow any weapons on our premises. Don't worry about the check. The meal is on us."

"Score!" Patrick is seemingly unfazed about being booted out of the place for waving around a switchblade, and more interested in the free meal.

"I'll call you later, Katie," he shouts just as I'm herded through the staff door.

There's a small corridor on the other side. To the left, I can hear the hustle and bustle of the restaurant's kitchen, but I'm led through a door on the right, into a small, neat office.

"Hey, are you okay?" Ben asks as he enters the room a few seconds later and wraps his arms around me, squeezing.

It's a little on the tight side, but honestly, I'm a bit shaken up by what just happened so I don't really mind.

My hands slide around his waist and I squeeze him back. My legs are tempted to join my arms, but I manage to control myself. I'm not sure what Ben would think if I suddenly started climbing him like a chimp scrambling up their favorite tree.

In spite of my great show of restraint, I realize that I'm fighting a losing battle. My feelings have taken root like an invasive strangler fig.

When Clem and Dan lived in Florida, they had a strangler fig whose long roots grew down along the trunk of the host tree, eventually completely engulfing the tree trunk until all you could see was a twisted mess of roots.

Those are my feelings for Ben. No matter how hard I try to get rid of them, they're not going anywhere. They are totally consuming me. Like a strangler fig.

"I'm fine, I guess. It was just a bit of a crazy way to end a crazy week. Thanks for rescuing me," I mumble into his chest. This is not the first time Ben's come to my aid. "You're becoming a regular knight in shining armor."

"Should I get a white horse?" Ben asks as he pulls away, much to my disappointment. I could stay glued to him forever.

I reluctantly leave the warmth of his chest just as the door opens.

"Is everything okay, Ben? I heard there was a man with a knife."

A man who looks in his early fifties is standing at the door, his concerned eyes darting between the two of us.

"Everything's okay. I'll fill you in later. Kate, this is Oscar Torres. He's the manager. Oscar, this is Kate. Mind if we use your office for a few minutes? We won't be long."

"Sure, no problem." He backs out of the room, quietly closing the door behind him.

"Are you sure you're okay? That guy was giving off some serious serial killer vibes. I was worried. I just about had a heart-attack when he pulled out the switchblade."

"I'm fine. Honestly. It was a bit of a shock, but I'm fine."

Actually, I'm *more than fine*, standing so close to Ben—but I'm not going to confess that. It will have him running for the hills.

"He doesn't know where you live or anything, right?"

"No! Of course not."

"Good girl," Ben says, pulling me back in for another hug. He runs his hands down my back reassuringly. It's very soothing. "I'm following you home though, just in case."

I have no objections. I love this sweet, protective side of Ben. Who am I kidding? I love *all* sides of Ben. There's really nothing about him that I don't like…other than the fact that he's not looking for a serious relationship, of course.

That reminder is like a bucket of ice water. I really have got to pull myself together.

"I walked here. It's not that far."

"In that case, I'm walking you home. There's no way you're walking back on your own. That psychopath could be waiting for you outside. I'm not taking any chances."

"That's sweet of you, but maybe you should check with the manager first. I mean, he seems like a reasonable guy, but I don't want you to get into any trouble."

Ben looks at me with furrowed brows, as if he's confused by what I just said. I'm not sure why. I feel like I monopolize so much of his time whenever I come here. I'd hate for him to get fired because of me.

"Uh…I'm not sure how I would get into trouble, but don't worry, I'll chat to Oscar."

And Ben does just that as we exit the office. Oscar is standing in the hallway. After a quick, hushed conversation, Ben puts his hand on my back and steers me outside.

"I'm taking the rest of the night off. Do you feel like watching a few more episodes of *Gilmore Girls*? We can finish season one. We get to see the epic scene where Max fills Lorelai's place with a thousand yellow daisies. It's one of my favorite episodes ever."

I know he's trying to distract me, just in case I'm really not okay, and I'm grateful. He is a lovely distraction. It's very amusing that he's not only watched all of the seasons of *Gilmore Girls*, but he can reference specific scenes. He's probably watched them multiple times. He sounds positively ecstatic about the yellow daisies' scene.

"I'm always up for watching *Gilmore Girls* with you, but I thought you shipped Lorelai and Luke, not Max?"

"I do. Lorelai and Luke are a perfect match. They were meant for each other, but it's still the best scene ever. When he proposes and she's surrounded by a sea of yellow daisies…" He puts his hand to his heart, like he's genuinely touched by the moment. "It's so romantic."

"Awww, Ben. You're just a little softy, aren't you?" I nudge him with my elbow. He's probably more romantic than me. It's cute.

"Hey! Less of the 'little', thanks." He flexes his bicep to prove his point before tucking my arm into his. "I'm a big, manly softy, thank you very much."

Before I can think better of it, I take the opportunity to rub his bicep with my free hand.

"Yep, definitely big and manly."

The moment the flirty words are out of my mouth I want to pull them back and shove them back down my throat.

Definitely big and manly? Really, Kate? Idiot.

Hopefully Ben can't see me blushing in the dark. The crimson shade is not just because of my awkward flirty remarks. There is something about this man's touch that does crazy things to me. I mean, it's just our arms linked, for goodness' sake. It's not like we're kissing, or even holding hands, so I'm not sure why my heart is beating so wildly in my chest.

Ben clears his throat.

"I was thinking…maybe you should pause this online dating thing."

Woah. He's jumping from serious, to playful, back to serious, so fast that it's giving me whiplash.

When I look at him, he's biting his lip again. It's very distracting.

"I already have a date lined up for next Friday, but after that, I'll consider it."

This time I don't mean the British version of "*I'll consider it*" which, along with *we'll see, perhaps, maybe,* and *could do,* really translates to NO. We're just too polite to say it.

No, this time I really will consider it.

Just thinking about the dead look in Patrick's eyes gives me the heebie jeebies. Alex will have a field day with this info, but I'm weighing up the pros and cons of telling my mum about this date. She'll have an absolute conniption.

Maybe I do need to reassess this whole online dating thing.

CHAPTER EIGHTEEN

"SO, 'OW was the date?"

I've barely had a chance to put away my things when Alex pounces.

This time, he's clever enough to sweeten me up in the form of coffee. Thank goodness he didn't attempt to make me tea.

I only have one cup of coffee a day, and the rest of the day I drink tea. I had to bring my own stash of teabags to work though, because everybody else drinks coffee. Alex has watched me make tea before, but I don't know how much information he actually absorbed in the process. At least coffee is a safe bet, and I accept it gratefully.

Viola sits down with her own cup of coffee just as I start filling Alex in.

"You're going to love this. He was a bit of a psychopath. Genuinely. If there was ever a date where I thought I might end up chopped up in pieces in somebody's basement, this was it."

Alex's eyes go wide. As much as he loves the drama, he would never want anything bad to happen to me.

"Did he threaten you? What 'appened?"

"No threats, but he was very creepy. I had this terrible feeling in my gut about him from the start. Something about him was just off. He was talking about how much he loved horror movies and then pulled out a switchblade and beheaded an ant.

"No!" Alex and Viola have exactly the same reaction.

"Yes! Right there at the table, mid-conversation. Sliced it in half. It was creepy."

"How frightening. Are you okay?" Viola looks very concerned.

"I'm fine. Thankfully Ben came to my rescue. He showed this guy the door and walked me home."

"Kate, are you sure it's a good idea to keep up with this online dating?"

"As I told Ben, I have a date set up for Friday, but after that, I'll have a think about it. It did give me a bit of a fright."

"I can set you up with those clients, or some single friends if you're interested. That's a much safer option than blind dates."

I'm sure my mother would like that option better too. When Mum and Dad called this weekend I was very vague about the details, much to Mum's disappointment. I just told her he was a bit creepy and had soulless eyes and left it at that. Thankfully she didn't push for more details because the "soulless eyes" bit got her nattering away about a new member of their bridge club. Apparently the old lady has soulless eyes too.

"Thanks, Viola. I'll let you know."

"Or, you could just date Ben," Alex chimes in.

"Sadly, that's not an option. I told you before, he's not looking for a serious relationship."

As I say it, I realize that the bartender thing really is a non-issue. Not since I've got to know how wonderful he is. I've been shallow and dismissive of people based on their work situation. Ben once told me that I shouldn't be so rigid that I let it stop me from missing out on something good. He *is* that something good. I don't care what job he has. I really could look past it. If only that was the only thing standing in our way. I also know that in spite of my first impression, he's not a player at all. He's kind, and thoughtful and utterly charming. He's every cinnamon roll hero I've ever loved. If only…

It hurts just thinking about it, so I distract myself by getting back to work.

***

"So have you still got just that one date lined up for this week?"

Ben's question as we're eating his famous spaghetti and meatballs on Monday night, doesn't surprise me. Since I arrived at his apartment for another *Gilmore Girls* marathon, I've been waiting for him to ask about the online dating thing.

"Yes, I haven't arranged anything else."

"And it's going to be at The Old Copper Pig again, right?"

"Yes."

"Have you got mace, or a rape whistle, or something?"

"Yes, Dad." I can't help the snarky response, but I'm secretly thrilled by Ben's overprotective line of questioning. He cares.

"Dad?" He raises an eyebrow. "Really? Um…I think you have me confused with somebody else. Does this look like a dad bod to you?"

He stands up and whips off his shirt, displaying those sexy abs I've only had a fleeting glimpse of up until now.

And *my, oh my*, are they delicious abs. I attempt to put up a façade of indifference, but my traitorous mouth pops open in appreciation of such sculpted perfection. I have no control over it.

I took an anatomy class once where my professor pointed out all the muscles. He could have used Ben as his model. If he had, I'm sure I would have passed with flying colors. Very educational.

Is that drool? I hope not.

I quickly wipe the corners of my mouth just in case.

"Nobody likes a show-off, Ben." I try to sound unaffected by the display of half-naked male perfection.

I actually really do like a show-off when they look like Ben. I *really really* do.

Ben's got my number though, because he smirks before pulling his shirt back on. There's something super sexy about that one-handed pull thing guys do when they're putting a shirt on.

"You know you love it, Callahan."

"Whatever, Fabio." I'm admitting nothing. "Let's just start watching the next season before I fall asleep here again."

***

If I thought Monday night was bad, our Wednesday night game night is equally as torturous. Partly because Ben opens the door just wearing running shorts.

Who does that?

It takes all of my willpower not to follow little beads of sweat as they make trails down his ripped body. Who would have thought sweat could be sexy? Not me, that's for sure.

"I'm just going to hop in the shower quick and then we can get started," Ben tells me.

This is some kind of sweet torture because I'm now imagining all the ways he and I can get started.

Does he realize how that sounds?

Hearing his shower running, knowing he's in there *naked*, is not helping the situation. I wonder if he's doing this just to mess with me?

I place the bag of tacos I picked up on the way on the kitchen island and browse through a cookbook that's sitting on the counter, in an attempt to distract myself.

"Smells good in here," Ben says as he rounds the corner, wearing nothing but plaid pajama bottoms that hang rather low on his hips.

I forcefully have to drag my eyes up from his chest to look at his face. His usual little smirk is in place.

"Enjoying the view?"

"No," I scoff. "Just thinking you might get cold. Aren't you going to put a shirt on or something?"

Ben laughs and disappears into his bedroom, returning with a shirt that he slips over his head.

"So, what are we playing tonight?" I ask as we dig in to the tacos.

"I thought we could do something a little different this time. We're gonna play *Fortnite*."

"*Fortnite*? Like the one where you shoot and build and stuff, while the circle closes in?"

"You know it?" Ben looks shocked.

"I've seen my eighteen-year-old cousin play it. Clem's youngest brother. I'm not sure I'm going to be any good. I don't think I can shoot a stationary target, never mind a moving one."

"Don't worry, we can practice. I'll show you how."

As it turns out, Ben doesn't need to show me how. If anything, I'm the one schooling him. I don't know what kind of sorcery this is, but I am freakishly good at shooting things. Not so much building, but I hide well enough to get down to the last five players in most of the games we play. I even win three rounds.

Poor Ben barely makes it into the top ten.

"Need some tips there, champ?" I tease, after I win my third round.

"I should have kept the shirt off," Ben grumbles.

CHAPTER NINETEEN

WHEN I walk into The Old Copper Pig on Friday night, I immediately spot my date because he's waving me over very enthusiastically.

As I make my way to the table I look around for Ben. He's not behind the bar, but I spot him sitting at a table with Oscar. There are papers spread out on the table in front of them and Oscar is talking very animatedly. It must be a staff meeting of some kind.

Just then Ben looks up and spots me. He gives me a quick wink before turning back to the papers in front of him.

It's not the first time he's winked at me. I've actually lost count of how many times he's done it, but every time, without fail, it feels like an invisible fist closes around my heart, tightening until I can hardly breathe. He's so handsome it hurts.

And a winking Ben? That should be illegal.

I really shouldn't be having these thoughts as I walk towards Frank. I'm a terrible date. Good thing he can't read my mind.

"Hello. It's nice to meet you, Kate. I'm Frank." He kisses each cheek French-style. I make a mental note of this especially for Alex.

Frank is nice looking, but his thick, dark hair is slicked back with a bit too much gel. It doesn't move an inch. You'd probably need a crowbar to make any changes to that hairstyle. It must take him hours to wash all that product off.

"Hi Frank. It's nice to meet you too. Hope you haven't been waiting for long."

I take a seat, noting that we've been seated at a spacious table for four, instead of the customary table for two I'm usually at.

It's probably because they're quite busy this evening, even if it is fairly early.

"Not at all. I was a few minutes early. My mother always drummed punctuality into me."

I'm pleased to hear this. Politeness and punctuality are the cornerstones of civilized society—at least my mother tells me they are.

"Your mother sounds like she would get on famously with my mum," I tell him.

"My mother is the best."

It warms my heart to hear a guy talk about his mom so sweetly. Especially a guy like Frank. He's not particularly tall, in fact he's a bit shorter than I normally like, but he has broad, muscular shoulders. He owns a boxing gym and has very similar interests.

As we chat over drinks, I realize that he's living up to the Italian American stereotype: he dotes on his mother and seems to have a loud, close-knit family.

Family is really important to me, so this makes me happy.

That is, until I catch the tail-end of a story about his mum that has my Spidey senses tingling. It seems like she's definitely the one making all the business decisions.

"Your mum works for you? Don't you get tired of being in each other's pockets all day?" I can't imagine it. Mum talks the hind leg off a donkey. She would drive me absolutely batty.

"I couldn't function without her. She keeps everything running smoothly."

"Oh, that's good. I love my mum but I couldn't work with her all day. At least you get a break at the end of the day," I say with a little laugh.

"Oh no! I live with my parents. I could never live without my ma." He looks at me like it's a given. "Who else is going to do my laundry and cook my meals?"

I'm not quite sure what to say to that. I'm tempted to ask if she picks out his clothes for him too, but the Brit in me would never allow me to be so rude.

"Does your mum not mind doing that?" *He's thirty-five!*

"I told you, there's nobody in the world like my ma. I'm her baby. She would do anything for me. She'll always be my number one. I'll never love any woman as much as I love my ma. *Never.*"

Well, that's a bright red flag if ever there was one! I don't mind a mama's boy, as long as they're still independent and not tied to the apron strings. He'll never love any woman as much as he loves his mother? That's a big NOPE from me.

"Oh, and here she is."

Here who is? I'm confused.

My confusion is quickly cleared up when I turn and see a lady in her late fifties walking towards the table.

"Kate, this is my mother, Isabella Rossi."

My brain stalls.

His *mother?*

"Uh…hi." I hold out my hand, still a little unsure of what's happening. She shakes it vigorously.

"I'm so excited to meet you!" Even with my untrained ear, I can hear her very distinct New York accent. "When my Frankie told me he was going on a date with a beautiful brunette I thought he was lying until he showed me your pictures. Gorgeous! Just gorgeous!"

Her accent is so strong it sounds like there is a W somewhere in "gorgeous".

She sits down at one of the empty chairs and grabs my hands that are clasped together on the table.

"I just *knew*, the minute I saw you! I said 'Frankie, this is the girl for you! I can feel it' and he said 'Ma, I hope you're right'. So I said to my Frankie, I was gonna come and meet you on this date. And I know what you're thinking, I know. This is a date. Who wants their ma, on their date? But, trust me, my Frankie relies on my advice, even if he won't admit it. He doesn't need my help when it comes to getting the ladies. He's a real charmer, he is. Like his father. But a ma wants to know that her son has a good woman. Somebody who's gonna look after him and care for him. He relies on my advice because I know what he needs. I just wanna make sure that if we're gonna welcome somebody as a Rossi, that they're really worthy of my Frankie. And you are honey! You are! Frankie, imagine how gorgeous she's gonna look in Nonna's wedding dress! Ah! I can't just picture it! Gorgeous!"

I'm sure I look like one of those cartoon characters with their eyes completely bugging out.

Frankie…I mean, Frank, is sitting there smiling at his mother, as if there is nothing unusual about this. As for his mother, she's still clasping onto my hands tightly and looking at me with a mixture of gratitude and admiration.

It's all a bit overwhelming.

Looking towards the table where Ben is sitting, I can see he has one hand fisted at his mouth and his eyes are closed. He looks a bit like he's praying. Or maybe he has indigestion.

As if he can sense I'm watching him, Ben opens his eyes. His eyes zero in on me for just a second before he quickly looks away. Not quick enough for me to miss the mischief that is dancing in them.

And then I see it. His shoulders are shaking. He's laughing! Or trying desperately not to, anyway. I'm not sure he's winning that battle because his face is turning crimson and his entire body seems to be vibrating with mirth.

Oscar stops talking and looks at Ben, who just shakes his head.

It's a comical sight, Ben, on the brink of an uncontrollable eruption, trying valiantly to silence the roaring laughter bubbling within him. He has obviously worked out who this lady is and finds it side-splittingly hilarious that a guy has brought his mother on a date.

And that thought sets me off. I start giggling like a teenager.

Mrs. Rossi is still holding onto my hands on top of the table. Her eyes bounce between me and Frank, looking more and more concerned the longer the giggles go on.

I can't help it. My eyes are starting to water.

"Is she okay?" Mrs. Rossi directs that question to Frankie.

"I'm sorry. I'm so sorry." I manage to get myself under control enough to blurt out an apology. If my mum could see me now, she'd be mortified by my manners. Horrified. Dad would probably laugh right along with me.

I take a deep breath to steady myself and make a point of not looking in Ben's direction, in case he sets me off again.

"Mrs. Rossi…"

"Isabella, please honey! Hopefully one day soon, 'Ma', huh?" She laughs and gives my hands another little squeeze. If I weren't meeting her under these strange circumstances, I'd actually find her quite delightful.

"Isabella…you're very kind, and your son seems very sweet." She elbows her son playfully and wiggles her eyebrows, obviously thrilled by the compliment. "It's just that, when I said I was looking for a serious relationship, I didn't mean I want to go racing down the aisle.

I just meant I wasn't looking for a casual hookup. You honestly seem like a wonderful lady, but meeting the mother on the first date…this is all just a little overwhelming."

"Oh honey! Say no more! I know you just want some alone time with my Frankie. I'll leave you two lovebirds in peace."

Mrs. Rossi stands up and gives my hands one last squeeze before kissing me on each cheek. She does the same to her son before leaving with a pep in her step.

"Isn't she great?"

Frank clearly sees nothing unusual about this.

"She's very…welcoming."

"I knew just from our text messages that you two would get along great. I had to get rid of the last girl because she said Ma was too much and interfered too much. Too much? A mother can never love her son too much. She said Ma was too controlling. *She* was the controlling one! She wanted me to move out of Ma's house! Can you believe it?"

I can believe it. I absolutely can.

I'm mentally composing the termination message right now.

CHAPTER TWENTY

"HELLO, darling."

It's always comforting to hear Dad's voice after an eventful week. He's a big teddy bear and I wish he was close enough to cuddle.

"Hello, Dad. How are the plants?"

"Thriving. The new gardener is working miracles. It's looking very colorful. We even had a game of bridge in the garden yesterday. Beautiful day. We're inching towards 'one leg out of duvet, constant pillow turning' temperature. Marvelous summer weather."

"Is that the bridge club that has a new member with soulless eyes?" I tease.

"Please don't get your mother started on that! She thinks she's some kind of detective. She's been watching too many of those *Midsomer Murder* reruns. Thinks she's a regular Miss Marple now."

"I think you've got the show and the character mixed up there, Dad."

I actually have no idea what Dad's on about, but I can hear Mum grumbling in the background.

"Never mind about that. This is perfect visiting weather, so when are you coming to visit?"

"Dad, I've only been here for three months."

"I know, but I'm missing my girl."

"Ah Dad, I miss you too. How's Mum?"

"She's right here. Chomping at the bit to find out how the latest date went. I'll leave you to it. I love you!"

"I love you too, Dad."

There's a little shuffle on the other end of the line before I hear Mum's voice.

"Hello, darling. So how did it go with the Italian American chap? Was he handsome? The Italians really know how to make some handsome babies. And very romantic. I once dated an Italian."

Oh boy. I'd better distract her in case she starts talking about twigs and berries again!

"He was nice enough, but his mum showed up too."

"His mum!"

I had been expecting the high-pitched shriek, so I had prepared myself by pulling the phone slightly away from my ear.

"Yes. He's very attached. She started talking about marriage and me wearing his Nonna's wedding dress."

"Oh good heavens! That's not a good sign, Kate! The last thing you want is an overbearing mother-in-law. Family man, yes, but not somebody who's attached at the apron strings. That's just asking for trouble."

Mum is absolutely right. I may tease her for being a drama queen, and the nosiest person I know (although Alex is right up there with her), but she would never dream of interfering in my relationships.

She proved that she can respect boundaries when I was dating Johnny. She told me privately that she didn't think he was good enough for me, but that it was my life, my choices and never said another word about it. She was always polite to him.

"I know Mum. Don't worry. We're not having a second date. I've already sent him the termination message. So, what's this about you being a detective?"

That was the perfect question to ask to get her off the topic of my love life, because she launches into a discussion that I can just imagine is very animated on her side of the phone.

"You know I told you about the new bridge club member, Prudence? The one with the soulless eyes?" She doesn't give me any time to respond. "Well, I went to visit your nan this week and while we were there, I saw an old lady with that same soulless look in her eyes. They could be related. I told your nan about it and she laughed so hard I thought she might have a little accident. She called the old duck over, and told her what I said! I thought I was going to die on the spot. I wanted to go to sleep and wake up in the next century…like that fairy tale. Anyway, the old duck laughed and then popped her one eye right out! Just popped it out right there. It was a glass eye! Well, I don't think they're really made of glass, but it was a prosthetic eye! That's why it looked soulless!"

Mum sounds thrilled by this information and I chuckle, imagining how the scene played out.

"The nurse saw her and scolded her, because apparently the doctor has told her several times she's not supposed to do it, but Nan says it's a bit of a party trick for the old duck. The one time she popped it out and it rolled. They spent an hour looking for it, only to find Arthur—you know, the one who's half blind—had thought it was a ping pong ball and had put it on the ping pong table. Luckily nobody actually played with it. Not sure it would have bounced very well. Nan said it was chaos and the old biddy got a right telling-off by the doctor."

This elicits more giggles from me. I wish I was close enough to visit Nan and hear all of her crazy care home stories.

"But how does that make you a detective, Mum?" I'm still not quite sure how the two things are linked.

"Well, now I'm thinking that perhaps Prudence doesn't have soulless eyes after all. Maybe she has a prosthetic eye that just gives her that look. But I can't outright ask her, because that would just be rude now, wouldn't it? So now I'm trying to use more stealthy methods of finding out."

"Oh boy, Mum. Please don't do anything illegal."

"Of course not, darling! I already assured your father that my methods will be above reproach. Aunty Dot is helping me brainstorm. It will be very clandestine."

This is not good news at all. Those two may look like unassuming, posh old ladies, but when they're together, they're trouble with a capital T. I can just imagine them waiting for Prudence to go out, entering her house uninvited, and having a good nose around.

"Nothing that could get you into trouble with the police, Mum!" I reiterate.

Mum sounds put out.

"Really, Catherine! Do you even know me?"

Yes. Yes I do. And that's the problem.

***

While I'm waiting for Ben to arrive for our *Gilmore Girls* night, I get a call from Claire, trying to set me up on a blind date with her coworker Jason.

"He's back from his trip. I promise you, he's an amazing guy. I showed him your picture and he's really excited to meet you. So, what do you say?"

I mentally run through the pictures we took and shared at dinner and the comedy club. I hope it wasn't the one where my head is dropped as I struggle to contain my laughter. I think I have about three chins in that photo.

"Sure, why not? Maybe Friday?"

If I'm going to find The One, I might as well take a chance. After my date with psycho Patrick, I realize this is probably a much better idea than some random person on an app. Claire worked with Jason for years and she assures me, he meets all of the requirements on my list. Although, truthfully, I'm feeling less and less enthusiastic about going on any dates. Perhaps because Ben takes up so much real estate in my head.

"Eeeeeeeeee! I'm so excited. You're going to love him! I'll give him your number."

I'm not sure I share her enthusiasm and when she hangs up, I'm already having second thoughts. I mean, I still want to find Mr. Right, but experience has proved that finding someone normal is harder than you think.

After all these bad dates, there'll always be a little niggling at the back of my mind that something is going to happen to leave a bad taste in my mouth. The guy that I actually have an interest in, is not interested in settling down. I wonder if anybody will ever measure up to Ben. Nobody makes my heart race like he does. Maybe I'm destined to be single.

Snap out of it, Kate. Nobody likes a whinger.

I'm hoping a little mental pep talk will help me snap out of the sulks. Thankfully the apartment buzzer distracts me from dwelling any longer on the sad state of my dating life.

"Hey, I brought dinner." As I open the door, Ben's smiling face instantly cheers me up. That and the smell of Chinese food. He knows me so well.

"My favorite! You're amazing!"

We make ourselves comfortable on the floor in front of the sofa, spreading the food out on the coffee table.

My phone buzzes on the table and I see it's a message from Claire, confirming Jason is free next Friday night for drinks. I tap out a quick response before tucking back into the Chinese.

"Planning another date?" Ben looks pointedly at the phone and the crease on his forehead jumps back into place.

He probably thinks I need my head read after what happened with Patrick. The only date I've had since then was with Frank last week, and that had been prearranged.

"Yeah, but don't worry, it's not on the app." I don't want him to think I went back on my word after I told him I'd give the online dating thing a break. "Claire has set up a date on Friday night with that guy Jason. Remember the one she mentioned at dinner? You've met him?"

Ben clears his throat before giving a short and sharp reply that's very unlike him. "Yes. He's…nice."

Only, Ben's tone of voice makes it sound like he's anything but nice.

There's an awful sinking feeling in my gut.

Ben is annoyingly optimistic about things…and people. I've never heard him say a bad word about anybody. And that includes Courtney the leech that had her hands all over him. Even when he's irritated and rejecting women's advances he's quite polite about it.

He had a few choice words about knife-wielding Patrick, but that doesn't really count. He's a really positive guy. But there's something about the way he acts whenever we talk about Jason that sends off warning bells in me. He was weird about it at the comedy club and he's being weird about it now.

"You would tell me if there was something wrong with him, right?"

"There's nothing wrong with him. Let's start the next season of *Gilmore Girls* before it gets too late." He reaches for the remote and starts the next episode without so much as a glance in my direction.

The rapid change of subject doesn't make me feel any better. So much for talking myself out of my doom and gloom mood.

CHAPTER TWENTY-ONE

WHEN Wednesday rolls around and Ben cancels our game night, I know that something is definitely up. Unfortunately, he's been avoiding me like the plague so I can't even ask him about it.

When I sent a text asking if everything was okay, all I got back was: **Busy week. We'll talk soon.**

We've messaged each other almost every day for a couple of months and now suddenly radio silence, and then *this*?

Ugh, males!

I know Ben well enough to know that something is wrong and it's exceedingly frustrating that he won't just tell me what it is.

I'm elbows-deep in a legal document on Friday morning when Alex's voice snags my attention.

"Hmmm. Interesting…"

I turn to see what he's looking at that is so interesting, only to find Ben striding towards my desk looking like a man on a mission.

"Hey. I was hoping to catch you on a lunch break so we could talk."

He flicks his gaze towards Alex, who's standing with his arms folded against our shared partition, unashamedly listening to our conversation.

"You must be Alex." Ben nods in his direction.

Alex starts giggling, but I completely ignore him.

"How did you even get past security?" I ask.

The building has a strict security policy because we occasionally have visits from our celebrity clients. They don't let anybody up without an appointment.

Ben shrugs. "I just asked."

I roll my eyes. Of course he did.

There's a female receptionist at the entrance to the building that acts as a gatekeeper. He's too gorgeous for his own good. He could charm the knickers off a nun.

"Sure. There's a coffee truck down the street. Maybe we can grab some and take a walk in the park," I say as I grab my purse.

It's been one of those days where I need more than one coffee.

Ben is quiet as I order coffee and by the time I get it, I'm just about tearing my hair out.

This is completely unlike him and I'm not just talking about the fact that he didn't want any coffee. From the very moment we met he's been so easygoing and friendly. He's become my best friend.

I've never once felt like he had his defenses up, but now I feel like he's a stranger. This feels more like one of my painfully awkward dates.

I'm just about to say something to him when he beats me to it.

"I can't let you go on this date tonight without telling you how I feel. I know you've been wondering about why I don't want to discuss Jason." The words burst out of him like he's in a hurry to get this off his chest.

I'm about to respond when he raises a hand to stop me.

"The truth is he's a great guy. Amazing, in fact. And that's the problem. I can't...I don't want you to fall for him."

He runs a hand through his hair in frustration, making it stick out in all directions.

"What? Why are you telling me this, Ben?"

I'm so confused. Why wouldn't he want me to be with a nice guy?

"I'm sorry. I'm messing this up, I know. Kate, I can't...I can't keep doing this."

I still have no idea what he's talking about. *Doing what?*

"I've wrestled with this for months. I've been trying to do the right thing at the right time. I don't want to be your friend or your wingman. I've fallen for you, Kate."

"Wait...You...you what?" Of all the things Ben could have possibly told me, this was the last thing I was expecting. A thrill runs through me at his words, but it also leaves me feeling completely bewildered. He's never even hinted at the fact that he might be interested in more. "But you don't…you don't want the same things as me."

"I was never in hurry to settle down because I hadn't met the right person. It was never about not wanting it; it was about timing. I was quite content with where my life was…until you. You walked up to the bar and turned my life upside down. I know you think we don't want the same things, but you're wrong. I'm head-over-heels in love with you. I have been for a while." He spreads his arms wide in a gesture that seems vulnerable. "I may not tick every box on your list, but this is me. And I want everything with you. I'm all in Kate."

My jaw is just about on the floor. He wants to settle down? With *me*? He's all in?

This is too much information for my brain to process. He locks eyes with me, his expression the most sincere and intense I've ever seen it. It feels like a laser beam penetrating directly into the depths of my soul. And I'm frowning in confusion, because he sounds nothing like the Ben I've come to know. The Ben who doesn't want a serious relationship.

When I just stand there, mouth open, staring at him like he just grew another head, he closes his eyes and shakes his head.

"I see. If you're going to break my heart, I'd rather not know right at this moment." He bites his bottom lip and chuckles nervously. "I know this was the worst delivery ever, I just needed you to know how I felt before you went on your date tonight."

And with that, he turns around and walks away from me.

I don't think I've ever experienced such a rollercoaster of emotions in such a short space of time: weariness, confusion, unadulterated joy, and now watching him walk away…sadness. I feel like a piece of my heart is walking away from me and I'm too dumbfounded to do anything except stand there with my mouth agape.

I don't know how long I'm immobile for, but by the time I manage to gather my wits, my coffee is cold. I walk back to the office in a trance and even Alex's probing questions can't shake me from this weird state.

I try to push away all the emotions that keep threatening to bubble up because I have work to do, but I feel like I'm walking through fog.

All afternoon I'm tormented by thoughts of Ben and how much of an idiot I am for being so utterly gobsmacked.

I'm self-aware enough to admit that I feel the same about Ben. In spite of all my mental pep talks warning myself he was off-limits, he somehow managed to wriggle his way right under my skin and into my heart.

And yet, that doesn't change the fact that he doesn't tick every box on my list.

He ticks the most important ones, though. Does it really matter if he's a bartender when he's kind, and funny, and generous? And he really *is* looking for something serious. My heart somersaults at that thought.

I'm also waging an internal war about what to do about drinks with Jason. Is it right to go for drinks with the guy when I've just admitted to myself that I have feelings for another guy? Is it better to cancel, even though it's at the last minute?

I take a deep breath and rub my hands down my face. Looking at the time on my phone, I see it's already almost the end of the day. I'm supposed to be meeting Jason in an hour.

It's only out of respect for both Claire and Jason that I decide not to cancel at the last minute, even though my heart isn't really in it.

***

Thank goodness we didn't arrange to meet at The Old Copper Pig. I'm not sure if Ben is working tonight, but after what happened today, it would just be cruel to wave this date right under his nose. Besides, if I did see him tonight, I might be tempted to climb him like a baby koala and plant a big smooch on his gorgeous lips. Then I'd be the bad date Jason tells all his coworkers about.

Instead, we're meeting for drinks at a little Irish pub not far from work. While it's a quaint little place, it doesn't have the same rustic urban charm that The Old Copper Pig has.

I push open the door, jamming it straight into a very solid back.

"Oh, I'm so sorry," I apologize as the unsuspecting victim of my door attack turns around. Thankfully, he's laughing.

"No worries." His face lights up as he takes me in.

"You must be Kate?" he says, holding out his hand. "Claire sent me a picture so I'd know who to look out for."

I once again say a silent prayer that it wasn't the double-chin picture. I'm sure Claire wouldn't be that cruel.

"Yeah. Sorry, again. That was a bit of a painful introduction."

"Not as painful as the time my date gave me a concussion." He grins.

I can't help but laugh. The levity of the situation helps to ease the heavy weight I'm feeling at the moment. I'm relieved Jason has a sense of humor about it.

"That sounds like a story I have to hear. We can commiserate about bad dates! Have you just arrived?" I ask.

"Yes. Perfect timing! Why don't you go grab us a seat and I'll get us something to drink?"

Jason is everything Claire said he would be and more. He's handsome, attentive, kind, funny and he has a great job. He is everything I'm looking for in a partner because he fits the list perfectly…and yet, my heart is just not in it. He's perfect in every way, except he's not Ben.

After he gives me a polite goodbye peck on the cheek, I drive straight to Clem and Dan's place.

***

Clementine opens the door, takes one look at my crumpled face, and says, "Oh, Kate."

That's all it takes for me to burst into floods of tears as the emotions I've been pushing down all day cascade to the surface. I launch myself into her arms.

Dan's watching television in the living room. He's about to say hi, but obviously swallows his words when he sees the expression on my face.

You know how some women can still look beautiful, even when they cry? That's not me. This is face-scrunching, snot-flying, ugly crying. And judging by the alarmed expression on poor Dan's face, he wants no part in this emotional display.

Clem leads me to their bedroom where we sit under the covers as I try to get my wracking sobs under control.

"So, are you going to tell me why my cool, controlled cousin has turned into a sniveling mess?"

I struggle to get the words out between the tears. "I think I'm in love with Ben."

"Of course you are." She doesn't sound a bit surprised by this news.

"Bu…But it's not sssssupposed to happen like this. He doesn't fit the—"

"If you say the word 'list' I'm going to shove it up your backside, Catherine Callahan. Oh Kate, you silly goose. That's why it's called *falling* in love. You can't force it to happen, you don't plan it, it just happens. Sometimes the best relationships are the ones you didn't expect to be in, the ones you never even saw coming. As much as you want to plan your life, it has a way of surprising you with unexpected things that will make you happier than you ever thought possible."

I know Clem speaks from experience.

"He does make me happy. *So* happy. He told me he's in love with me," I say, using the back of my hand to wipe at my face.

"Then what's the problem, you numpty? He loves you, and you love him. Toss the list and just do what makes you happy, Kate. Come on, dry your eyes. Nobody wants to see you ugly cry. Besides, I don't want you to get any snot on my new duvet."

Clem rubs the duvet cover lovingly before handing me a Kleenex. Her no-nonsense approach makes me laugh a little. So typically Clem.

Just then I feel my phone vibrate in my pocket. Pulling it out, I see it's a message from Ben.

Ben: Please can we forget what I said today? I don't want to lose the most important thing to me. Even if it just means being friends.

Well now that sucks. Because I was too dumbfounded to say a thing, he thinks I don't feel the same. Before I can think of a suitable reply, the phone pings again.

Ben: How was the date?

With that message I feel like my heart is going to explode. It's a message he's sent to me dozens of times, but it must be killing him to ask this time. I know he's only doing it because he wants me to be happy and that just makes my heart hurt for him. He's too good for me.

I can't leave him on read, but I don't want to pour my heart out over text message either so I keep my reply simple: **Unremarkable.**

"So how do I fix this, Clem?"

"You need to come up with some grand romantic gesture. When do you see him again?"

"Probably on our Monday Movie Night. That's if he doesn't cancel."

"Great. Then we have the whole weekend to plan."

Clementine cups her hands around her mouth and shouts to the other end of the house, "Dan, Kate's staying. You're sleeping in the spare room tonight!"

"Hey now." I try to hush her. "Did you forget you have kids?"

I'm expecting to hear wails from their bedroom any second now after their mother was screeching like a banshee.

She waves off my comment. "Don't worry, once they're down, they sleep like the dead. It's a good thing too because this bed squeaks like a rusty swing set in a windstorm." She wiggles her eyebrows.

"CLEMENTINE!" I cover my ears in case she decides to add anything else. "TMI. I do NOT need that mental image! And now you want me to sleep in this bed?"

Clem laughs and pulls my hands away from my ears. "Oh don't be such a prude. You can relax. I changed the sheets today."

I shake my head and get back to the topic at hand. "So…a grand gesture, huh?"

Clementine rubs her hands together and I can see from the twinkle in her eye that she's excited about us cooking up a plan.

CHAPTER TWENTY-TWO

I'M STANDING in Ben's living room, fidgeting nervously while I wait for him to get back home. Thank goodness Will not only had a spare key for Ben's place, but was also a good sport about letting me in to set up the surprise.

When Clem asked me what some of Ben's favorite things were, I just knew I had to use *Gilmore Girls* as inspiration. Ben is just a big romantic softy and I'm hoping that this grand romantic gesture is enough to get him to: A, forgive me for standing there silently like a doofus while he professed his love, and B, understand how head-over-heels I am for him too.

There is, of course, a tiny chance he may think it's creepy that I snuck into his apartment without his permission or knowledge, but I'm willing to take that chance.

This is why, for the entire weekend, Clementine and I drove in different directions around the state buying all the yellow daisies we could find. We even roped Dan in on the hunt. I've spent enough to fund the budget of a small country but it's worth it. Perhaps slightly irresponsible, but still worth it.

It's supposed to be one thousand, but actually it's closer to three thousand because that's what happens when three different people are trying to buy up all the daisies they can find. The room still doesn't look nearly as full as Lorelai's place, but we've arranged them on different surfaces at different heights in the living room so it still looks pretty spectacular.

The three of us (and Will, bless him) have spent the past hour lugging buckets of yellow daisies up three flights of stairs. On any other day I would be ready to pass out from all the stair-climbing, but I'm too wired. I feel like I've been hooked up to a caffeine IV for the last hour. I'm a jittery mess.

"It looks fab. Are you all set?" Clem asks.

"I think so." I rub my sweaty hands against my legs.

I don't know why I'm so nervous. I mean, I know that Ben feels the same. It's not like I'm going in blind and making this grand romantic gesture without any idea of how he feels, but the chronic overthinker in me can't help but feel anxious. What if he's changed his mind in the last few days? Maybe he's decided we'd actually be better off as friends. Or maybe he's not going to take me seriously. He knows about the list. I don't want him to ever think I'm just settling and that he's not my first choice.

"Okay, then I'm going to head out. The take-out is on the kitchen counter."

It was my turn to bring the food for our Monday Movie Night. Thank goodness for Clem, because in my anxiety over the daisies and getting everything ready, I had actually forgotten all about it. Darling, on-the-ball Clem sent Dan out earlier so by the time I realized my mistake, he was already walking into the apartment with the food.

"Thanks Clem. Not just for all this." I wave my arm around at the yellow daisies that fill the room. "But for everything."

"Aw, anytime my little chicken nugget. What are cousins for?" She gives me a hug before she leaves, closing the door behind her.

Just then, I get a text message from Oscar giving me a heads up that Ben has left work, which is just around the corner. Getting the manager's phone number was no easy feat. Will had to ask a friend, to ask another friend, to ask a waitress he used to date who works at The Old Copper Pig. Thankfully Oscar was very excited when I explained my plan.

When I texted him earlier in a panic because I was worried we wouldn't be able to get everything set up in time, he said he'd stall Ben at work for an extra thirty minutes. It's amazing what people will agree to do for a good love story. I owe Will, Dan and Clem, and Oscar. I wonder how they feel about yellow daisies.

There is a jangle of keys in the door and I hold my breath. This is it.

Ben opens the door and takes one step before coming to an abrupt halt. His eyes widen as he takes in the thousands of yellow daisies, and me standing in the middle.

"Don't worry, I'm not going to propose." I don't know why that's the first thing that comes out of my mouth but it makes Ben chuckle. He places his keys on the console in the entrance before pinning me with his intense gaze.

"So why did you do this, Callahan?" Ben asks as he walks towards me slowly, his eyes fixed on mine. The small grin on his face tells me he already knows exactly why I did this. But he needs to hear the words. He deserves to hear the words.

"Because I wanted to do something to show you that I'm completely in love with you. Because I need you to know that me keeping quiet on Friday wasn't because I didn't feel the same, I was just in shock. I did it because I want you to know that you are everything I could have ever hoped for and more. There's no uncertainty. You're better than any list."

Ben smiles and cups my face with his hands, wiping a tear from my cheek before he rests his forehead against mine. I hadn't realized I was crying.

"And I don't care that you're a bartender. I just love you for you."

Ben knows that a stable job was high up on my list, so I feel like it's important that he knows I really don't care about that. He is so much more than what job he does.

He doesn't say anything, but he presses a tiny kiss to the corner of my mouth. The touch is so fleeting and light, I would have wondered if I'd imagined it, if it weren't for the shivers it sends through me.

When his nose rubs gently against mine, my eyes flutter closed and I breathe him in. My senses are heightened, making me fully cognizant of every touch: the feel of his fingers in my hair, the pad of his thumbs as they stroke my cheeks, his warm breath caressing my face, and the press of his body against mine.

When he finally closes the whisper of space between us and kisses me properly, I feel like Alice, tumbling down the rabbit hole into Wonderland.

Boy does Ben know how to kiss. He devours my mouth as if he needs it to survive. As if he can't live without it. There is nothing sweet or soft about this kiss. It's an explosion of emotions that have been squashed down for too long. Like a bottle of soda that has been shaken and quickly opened. And I can do nothing but hold on and enjoy the ride. And enjoy it, I do. There is something utterly magical about kissing Ben.

When we finally stop making out like teenagers and come up for air, Ben says "Wow!" and laughs, before pressing a kiss to my forehead.

"I love you too, Kate. I think this is the best day of my life."

I giggle. I'm not sure if it's happiness, or relief. Perhaps a mixture of both.

While we're sitting on the floor of the living room eating the Vietnamese food Dan brought, Ben looks around at the daisies and nods in appreciation.

"You did good, Callahan."

"I knew you'd love it. You really are a romantic softy."

"Only with you." He leans over and kisses my cheek. "Oh, and by the way, I'm not a bartender."

I'm so surprised by his statement that I swallow a piece of chicken whole, which makes me cough. I quickly gulp down water before turning my confused face towards him.

"What do you mean you're not a bartender? I've seen you working behind the bar!"

"Yeah, I like to help out behind the bar. It gives me a chance to people-watch. I own The Old Copper Pig."

"You own it?"

"Yeah. Well, my brothers and I own it, although they're really silent partners."

"No wonder you said the boss was so amazing." I roll my eyes with a grin, thinking back on that very first conversation. He was talking about himself! The cheeky chap. "Why didn't you tell me?"

"It never really came up. I wasn't actually sure what you thought, but if you were under any misconceptions, I thought you'd realized I owned it the first night you came to my apartment. Not sure a bartender could afford an apartment like this."

"I thought Jackson got you a deal like mine!"

Ben laughs. "No. I guess now is also the time to tell you that the restaurant is only one of many pies I have my fingers in. I'm primarily a property developer. The apartment building you live in? That's one of my developments."

"You own the entire building?"

"Yeah. Well, for now at least. We'll sell off the apartments one by one once the renovations are complete."

I suck in a shocked breath.

"You're loaded!"

My mother would be horrified at my brazen reference to his financial state. She thinks talking about money is crass, but I can't help it. I'm totally astonished.

Thankfully Ben isn't at all offended. In fact, his boisterous laughter fills the air as his body shakes with unbridled amusement at my statement. His eyes still sparkle with mirth as he grabs the back of my head and plants a solid, smacking kiss on my lips. I'm not sure what's so funny…although I think perhaps it has more to do with my shocked expression than what I blurted out.

"I'm certainly not hurting for money," he says with a big smile.

Ben moves the cartons of food out of the way, pulls me up onto the couch next to him, and grabs the TV remote.

"So, are you ready for more Gilmore Girls, Callahan?" he asks as I snuggle into his chest. He's so comfy.

"I'm ready."

But he doesn't turn on the television. Instead, he's just holding the remote in mid-air.

"Hmmm."

His pause makes me look up at his face. His forehead is creased in thought.

"What is it?"

"I guess I'm going to have to stop calling you Callahan and find a new nickname."

"Why? I like it. Nobody else calls me that." The thought of him not calling me that makes me a bit sad.

"Well, if I have my way, you won't be a Callahan for that much longer."

He kisses my stunned face before turning back to the TV and putting on our show.

Not a Callahan for too much longer?

The thought makes me giddy with excitement. I should feel terrified at the thought of moving so fast, but I don't. He is it for me. There are no questions. No doubts. There is just Ben, and in the deepest part of me, I know that he is my forever.

EPILOGUE

BEN

"ARE YOU sure you're ready for this?" Kate looks at me with a teasing grin. She's warned me that her mother can be a little bit overbearing.

"Ready as I'll ever be, Angel." I can't resist giving her a quick kiss on the cheek before we get out of the car.

The truth is, I'm actually pretty nervous about meeting Kate's parents for the first time. I've joined in on a few of the Sunday calls since we started dating, but this will be the first time we meet in person.

Before we even get three steps from the car, the front door swings open and Felicity Callahan comes bounding out of the house, with arms open wide.

"Catherine, darling! I'm *so* happy you're finally here. I've been counting down the hours." She squeezes Kate so hard I hear the air whoosh out of her in a little choke, before Felicity turns her attention to me.

"And Benjamin. You're even more handsome in person."

She squeezes me just as tightly. Thankfully Felicity is fairly rotund and well-padded, to cushion things, otherwise I think she may have done some serious damage to my bones. She's a lot stronger than she looks.

"Give the poor chap some room to breathe, Floss!" Harold

admonishes his wife, before giving Kate a hug, and me a firm handshake.

"I brought you each a gift. Just a little something to say thanks for having us."

I suggested getting a hotel room while we're in England, but Harold and Felicity wouldn't hear of it.

"Oh, how kind! Isn't that kind of him Harold?" Felicity takes the gift bags I'm holding out. "Let's go out back for a cup of tea. It's unseasonably warm for October this year. We must enjoy it while we can."

It appears that Felicity is just as organized as Kate is because there's already a tea tray on the table.

Harold, Kate, and I take our seats as Felicity fusses over the tray.

"I know you don't drink tea Ben. Would you like some coffee?"

I'm about to say "Yes, please" but I look past Felicity and see both Harold and Kate furiously shaking their heads at me. It's a good thing Felicity has her back to them. So I guess that's a *no*, then? Thankfully there is also water on the table.

"I'll just have water, thank you."

Harold and Kate both look immensely relieved. I raise my eyebrow in question but Kate just blows me a kiss.

When Felicity has poured the tea she sits down and opens the gift bag.

"It's Caroline Graham's *Midsomer Murders* boxset! Look, Harold."

He just makes a non-committal noise and carries on sipping his tea.

"You know…Detective Barnaby. Thank you Ben. It's perfect!" She rubs her hand lovingly over the books that Kate assured me would be a big hit with her mom, who is an avid fan of murder mysteries. "Well, let's see what Ben got you then. Go on, open it."

Felicity shoves the bigger gift bag towards Harold. It was much harder to find something I thought he'd like. Kate gave me a list (she still loves her lists) of all his hobbies and interests to spark some ideas. It took a while, but I think he'll like what I've chosen.

"Oh look! A bird box kit with wireless camera. I've read all about these. You can watch the chicks hatch from your phone. Thank you, Ben."

"You're welcome. Kate said you enjoyed birdwatching. I'll help you set it up in the garden later, and we can link the camera in the box to your phone."

"What a thoughtful gift, Ben. He's not just a handsome face." Felicity directs the last part to Kate.

"I can see where Kate gets her charm from, Mrs. Callahan."

Felicity giggles at the compliment. "Please, call me Floss, dear. Everybody does."

"Yes, Mum. He's handsome and thoughtful, and very generous. I'm a lucky girl."

A warmth brightens Kate's features as she speaks, looking me directly in the eyes. I have to fight the urge to lean over, grab her face, and kiss her until we both can't breathe. I know from our vast experience of making out like teenagers, that we're very, very good at it. It's only out of respect for her parents that I'm still seated.

"Much better than that lay-about, Johnny, you used to date."

Kate's already told me all about useless Johnny. The guy must have been blind not to see what he had in Kate.

"Mum!" She rolls her eyes. "Nobody has any interest in hearing about my ex-boyfriends."

Her dad is still fiddling with the bird box, paying no attention whatsoever to the conversation around him.

Instead of dropping the subject, Felicity turns towards me again.

"All I'm saying is he was a lazy, inconsiderate bloke. Definitely a few cards short of a full deck. We already like you a million times better, dear." Felicity pats my hand.

"Thanks, but I'm actually the lucky one."

She clutches the pearls at her neck. "Ah, Harold, did you hear that? Young love. So romantic. Do you remember when we used to be so romantic, Harry?"

"No. I don't." Harold's deep baritone laugh rumbles through the air, before he goes straight back to his bird box. I scored some great points with that. I'm going to need them later.

Felicity just shakes her head, tutting in disapproval before asking about our plans for the next two weeks.

***

Later that afternoon, Harold and I are walking around the large garden, looking for the best spot for the bird box. You can see Kate's dad has a passion for gardening because his garden is a masterpiece. It's awash with autumn colors. It's beautiful, even in October. Unfortunately, Kate hasn't inherited his green fingers. She's already killed three houseplants and I've given up all hope.

"Uh, Mr. Callahan, while we're alone, I wanted to ask…well, I was hoping that…" I clear my suddenly scratchy throat and wipe my sweaty hands, trying to compose myself. I don't think I've ever fumbled over my words like this.

Harold gives me a knowing look.

"Yes, son. The answer is yes." Harold gives me a pat on the shoulder and just keeps walking.

"Uh." It takes a second for my brain, and then my body, to catch up.

Harold laughs at the expression on my face.

"I thought I'd put you out of your misery, son. Looks like you were struggling there a bit."

"You're really okay with me proposing to Kate?" I had this whole speech planned. This is not really going the way I expected it to. I thought it may take some convincing, considering how fast everything has happened. "I know we've only been dating a few months but I love your daughter, more than anything. From the first conversation we ever had, I just knew deep in my soul that I would never be the same because something big and life-changing was about to happen. I'm not gonna lie, Sir, I fell hard and fast. I don't blame you if you're worried about how fast everything is moving, but I want you to know that I don't have a shred of doubt in me. I promise you, that until the day I die, I'll protect and love your daughter. She is my life."

If you had asked me eight months ago whether I believed in love at first sight I would have given you a definitive "no". But then she walked in. And everything changed.

Sometimes love creeps up slowly, but sometimes it walks right up and punches you in the gut. That's what it was like with Kate: gut-punching, knock-you-right-out kind of love. The day we went to dinner after baseball, I just *knew* this was it for me. I looked across the table at this kind, strong, beautiful girl and I just knew.

Harold shakes his head as we continue our slow stroll.

"I'm not worried Ben. I've seen how you love her. You make her laugh like nobody else can. She's told us about some of the small things you do to make her life easier. You don't just *tell* her you love her. You show her. She's…lighter when she's with you. You're good for her, and I know she loves you too which is why it's so easy to say yes."

"Thank you, Mr. Callahan."

"Please, it's Harold. And you don't need to thank me. Loving my baby girl the way you do is thanks enough."

When we get back inside the house Felicity flaps around me like a mother hen, checking if I'm comfortable, if I need anything, if I want anything to eat or drink before we go to the care home to visit Kate's grandma.

"For heaven's sake, Floss. Give the man some breathing room. You're suffocating him."

"Nonsense. He's our guest. It's my job to look after him," she says, patting my chest. "Have fun with Nan, you two."

As we walk to the door, Harold whispers conspiratorially. "Are you sure you want her for a mother-in-law? It's not too late to back out." He laughs heartily at his own joke.

"Don't worry. I know what I'm signing up for," I whisper back confidently. Kate has been very informative on that front. Honestly, her mother is a real hoot.

At that pronouncement, Harold tips his head back and laughs uproariously. He shakes his head and pats me on the back, sending the silent message that I have no idea what I'm in for.

"What are you two whispering about?" Kate asks as she catches up with us, linking her arm with mine.

"Nothing you need to worry your pretty little head about," Harold replies. "Have fun with Nan. Don't let her get into any brawls!"

He closes the door behind us as we walk to the car.

Kate gives me a look that tells me she's dying to know what we were whispering about, but I don't want her to get any ideas so I sidetrack her with a question of my own.

"So, why don't I want to accept coffee from your mother?"

Sidetrack successful. Laughter bubbles out of Kate and it's like music to my soul. I love hearing her happy.

"Because Ben, there are many things my mother is very proficient at, but making coffee is not one of them." Her eyes sparkle with amusement.

"I thought even a bad cup of coffee was better than no coffee."

"Well, whoever came up with that saying has obviously never tasted Mum's coffee."

When we reach the car, instead of opening her door, I push Kate up against it, nuzzling my nose against hers before I find her mouth.

When my lips begin to move against hers, coaxing her to do the same, it doesn't take much convincing. She loops her arms over my shoulders and her hands quickly find my hair as she deepens the kiss, until we have to pull apart or risk passing out from insufficient oxygen.

"You know my nosy mum is probably watching through the window?"

"Well then, I hope she enjoyed the show." I laugh as Kate blushes at the thought of her mother witnessing us making out like hormonal teenagers.

I kiss her on the nose before opening her door. One thing I'm certain of is that I'll never get enough of this beautiful girl. When it comes to Kate, forever isn't long enough.

***

KATE

"I don't want you to get a shock when you meet Nan," I warn Ben. For the thousandth time. "She may be ninety, but she's a feisty old thing."

"Relax, Angel. You said she had a wicked sense of humor. I've got her the perfect gift." He holds up a small gift bag as we walk towards the entrance of the care home where Nan lives. "She's gonna love me."

I know she will. All the ladies do. I'm not worried about Nan not liking Ben. Just the opposite. She's the biggest flirt. I'm worried she's going to scare the poor guy off.

My fears are confirmed when Nan starts flirting the moment they're introduced.

"This is for you, Margaret." Ben hands her the small gift bag.

"You might as well call me Nan too, handsome. I would say you shouldn't have got me anything, but I love presents, so I won't."

Ben never told me what he'd got, only that it was a gag gift because I'd told him she loves them. What I do know is that he searched for weeks for the perfect gift.

"What do we have here?"

Nan pulls out a small book and flips it the right way around to read the title. And then she starts laughing. And laughing. A wheezing, chesty laugh that makes me concerned she's going to stop breathing altogether. The more she flips through the pages, the more she laughs, until she has tears running down her face.

Even Ben looks a bit alarmed at how forcefully she's laughing.

"What on earth did you get her?"

I take the book from Nan's hands and read the title: *Pilates on the Potty*. Flipping through the book, I see it's filled with illustrations of exercises to do to get fit…while on the toilet. Mum would be horrified, but Nan absolutely loves it. It's the perfect gift for her and I roll my eyes because it's so silly, but what I really want to do is cry from happiness knowing how much thought he's put into all of these gifts.

When Nan has calmed down enough to speak, she squeezes Ben's cheek.

"You're handsome *and* funny. If I were fifty years younger I'd run off with you, but seeing that I'm not, Kate will have to do."

"Uh. Thanks, Nan," I say, slightly offended. "I'm glad you managed to get yourself under control. I was worried we'd have to start CPR with the way you were wheezing."

"Maybe I should have kept on laughing then. I wouldn't mind getting mouth-to-mouth from your handsome beau."

"Nan!"

"I was more worried she was going to pop out a third boob again," Ben chimes in, obviously recalling the hernia story I'd told him.

His comment just sets Nan off again. Thankfully, this time she manages to compose herself a lot quicker.

"Yes, we definitely need you in the family, handsome. When are you putting a ring on it?"

"Nan! We've only been dating a few months. Give the poor guy a break."

"Don't worry, Nan. I'm working on it," Ben tells her with a wink.

"Hey, Edna," Nan shouts as the old duck walks past. "Come and meet my new grandson. He's much more handsome than that freckle-face boy who comes to visit you."

"Nan! Stop it!" I shush her. She's going to get into another brawl with Edna; I can feel it. "Don't be rude. If you don't behave, Ben and I are going to leave."

Thankfully Edna's as deaf as a doorpost these days and doesn't seem to have heard the insult.

"Okay, don't get your knickers in a knot, girl." She raises her hands in surrender. "She's far too uptight, this one," she adds for Ben's benefit. "You're going to be good for her, I can tell."

Nan gives Ben another pat on the cheek. I think it's just because she likes touching his face. I can't blame her. It is a very handsome face.

"So how did you end up falling in love with my granddaughter?"

"Well, Nan. It all started with a fart…"

"Ben!" I cannot believe Ben just said that. I think my face is beet red.

"Really? Now this sounds like my kind of story," Nan says, eager for more details.

"Yup, she tooted and I was an absolute goner. Not literally, although it was touch-and-go there for a moment."

"BEN!" I bury my face in my hands.

Nan is of course having another laughing fit.

"You're going to pay for that." I send Ben a dirty look.

"I look forward to any punishment you dish out, Angel," he says with a smirk.

I should have guessed that him and Nan would be trouble together. It makes my heart happy to see her laugh so much though.

Thankfully he does show me some mercy and changes the subject.

As Nan and Ben chat easily, I think about how fortunate I was to walk into The Old Copper Pig all those months ago. The truth is that Ben was already a goner long before that eventful car ride.

I once asked him why it took so long to tell me how he felt. He told me that he fell so hard, and so fast that it terrified him. The day we went to dinner after the Red Sox game, he *knew* I was it for him. But he also knew that he needed to hold back because he couldn't risk scaring me off by confessing too much too soon. I'm glad he did, because even though I may have been crushing on him hard, it took me a lot longer to be honest with myself about how deep those feelings really ran.

As if he can sense me watching him, Ben turns to me with eyes aglow with love. His warm hand envelopes mine, and I'm filled with a kind of contentment I only ever feel with him. He's all I need. He's everything.

THE END

AUTHOR'S NOTE

143

Dear reader,

Thank you for reading Kate and Ben's book. I hope you enjoyed reading it as much as I enjoyed writing it.

Boston is a beautiful city that has a special place in my heart. Although I no longer call it home, I will always be charmed by the history, architecture, and people. I hope that the books in this series give readers just a small taste of Boston's magic.

Look out for Noah and Viola's story, *The Race Track Ruse*.

For updates as well as free bonus chapters and books, please visit www.jillyduplessis.com and sign up for my newsletter.

With love,

Jilly

ABOUT THE AUTHOR

Jilly du Plessis is a firm believer in happily-ever-afters.
When she's not writing sweet romantic comedies, she's reading,
spending quality time with family and trying not to kill her house
plants. She holds a postgraduate degree in English. At various
times in her life Jilly has called America, Canada, and South Africa
home. She lives with her husband, two daughters, five crazy guinea
fowl, and not enough bookshelves.

www.ingramcontent.com/pod-product-compliance
Lightning Source LLC
Chambersburg PA
CBHW021000160726
47994CB00006B/2310